At Night, Outside The Window

Chapter I

The three storied farm house stood against the late afternoon sky as we approached on horseback. The shadows, which would soon put the building into silhouette as the sun sank into the western horizon, hid the fading, flaking and dirty paint, the broken windows, and the rest of the evidence of disrepair due to years of abandonment. All I felt was numb upon seeing the house again, after all these years.

"Are you alright, Joseph?" The older man's lean face with the neatly trimmed, graying beard beneath his wide brimmed hat, turned to me. I think he was the only soul to ever call me by my full name, rather than Foggy headed Joe, or just by my surname, MacReady.

The voice beside me speaking with a still noticeable German accent startled me, making me pull on the reigns too tightly, causing my mount to whiny with surprise and stray from the dusty road. In a soft voice, I coaxed the horse to settle down as he turned in a circle and shook his maned head, his hooves clomping about the broken rock amid the sage brush, and the half dried grass that was everywhere in this part of eastern Washington. I still recall the sense of chilly fright run down my spine. Had I meant to ride off like a scared rabbit at that moment before? Maybe.

"Yeah… Yes." I nodded my head, perhaps too quickly and eagerly to be believable. Mr. Gustaff Kahl, who I had been working for as a hand at his place for the past several months, regarded me with a smile and a quizzical furrow of his brow. "Sorry," I chuckled, "I was kinda drifting off in my own thoughts there for a space." I didn't think my explanation came off as particularly convincing, either.

Mr. Kahl, who had bought up a spread since arriving from South Dakota last year, had been living in the bunkhouse with the rest of us cowboys and harvest bums who he had hired on, till he could build a modest house for his daughter and himself. And then he learned from another Russian German wheat farmer who owned acreage next to his that the old, uninhabited house at the edge of his land was actually part of his property. The house had been empty for over fifteen years, with only tramps and hobos staying for the night before moving on to find work on a farm or ranch, or jump a train to greener pastures.

Why build a house, Mr. Kahl had reasoned as he ate lunch with us hands in the bunk house earlier in the day, when there was one that only needed fixing up? With sweat streaking our dirty faces and soaking our clothes from working since morning, all six of us had been ready to eat the cattle we had been branding, and the rye we had seeded in the fields we had just tilled. The boss had figured he could bring his daughter, who was staying with his in-laws back in Yankton, South Dakota, to Washington that much sooner. Some of the men between spoonfuls of pork and beans and sips of beer, joked about how everyone around here thought the place was haunted. Gotta love the Germans for their appreciation of beer.

Remaining quiet, I thoughtlessly stirred my beans about the plate, my appetite having vanished as memories, that I had wanted to be forgotten since I was a kid, came back to me. Mr. Kahl had guffawed out loud at the idea of bogeymen and spooks living on his property without paying rent. That was when Charlie McMurty, the burly cow puncher with jet black hair and facial stubble that seemed to defy any razor, and the biggest horses ass I knew, had raised his voice as he pointed at me, "Foggy headed Joe over here grew up around these parts," he sputtered half chewed food as he talked. "He knows all about it." He well knew all the stories about me. I'm a big man, but I've never been much of a fighter, and McMurty knew that when he'd needle me, or went out of his way to make me look stupid.

The other three hired men had turned their faces to me. A dark colored Spokane Indian named Gary, with his black hair cut short, who worked on local ranches and farms, was local, too. But McMurty would never have given him or any of his people credit for knowing anything, let alone giving them the time of day. The other two were hobos, Cranston and Juliani respectively. Skinny in their loose fitting overalls, and with faces haggard and worn before their time, they had been booted off a freight train by a rail yard bull, and had been looking for any work now that their means of transportation was gone.

Mr. Kahl took a drink of beer, so as not to spit pork and beans on us as McMurty had, before he spoke. "Well, while I'm always certainly interested in ghost stories, I'd actually prefer some company who knows the way when I take a look at the place today."

I cleared my throat before answering in a quiet voice: "I got a lot of work tying me up, here." I kept my gaze down on my dinner. "I don't think I can leave it undone."

I didn't need to look at Mr. Kahl to see the stunned expression on his face due to the sudden silence among my fellow hands. McMurty snickered and elbowed one of the scrawny harvest bums seated next to him, while everyone else fell silent and held their breath, expecting me to get a good bitching out at the very least. That had been till Mr. Kahl's burst of laughter allowed for sighs of relief and chuckles around the dinner table.

Reaching across the other side of the table, the Russian German settler jostled me by my shoulder. "I like a man who loves to work," he said with merriment, his face cracking in a grin. "But you forget,

I'm the boss, and if I say you ride with me instead of working, then you get the day off!"

"Lucky bastard," Juliani had muttered with a good natured, sideways grin as he eyed me.

Yeah, I was so lucky. That afternoon, Mr. Kahl and I had saddled our horses, and rode the length of his spread till we reached the house closer to evening.

Mr. Kahl climbed off his horse, and led the animal to a small stable outside the house. I did the same, my nerves feeling jittery just for being here. The bare wood of the building had since turned gray with rain, snow, and generally shitty weather, and sunlight streamed through the gaps above from where the roof had fallen in. Absentmindedly, I kicked pieces of wood away as my boss did as I followed him, seeing the rusted nails sticking out of parts of the roof that had once been nailed together. Tying off our horses, I followed him out toward the house. The broken windows looked inward to blackness. Local boys, me included, used to throw rocks at those windows. I really can't remember if we were trying to drive away the ghosts we thought were inside, or were daring them to come out. Hell, in all likelihood, we just wanted to see glass break.

"So, besides this place being haunted," Mr. Kahl asked, looking up at the balcony above on the third floor, "what's the story?"

"There isn't much I actually know," I answered truthfully, as I took off my hat to run my hand over my sweaty hair. "A fella from Hungry..."

"Hungary," Mr. Kahl corrected me, patiently.

"Yeah… A fella from Hungary set down roots almost twenty years ago. I heard tell he knew some English, but had lots of money."

"Uh huh." Mr. Kahl nodded, eyeing the house' facade as he climbed the steps up to the veranda that was held up by columns carved to look like they were from Greece, and approached the front door. The boards creaked under his boots. I trailed behind him, praying that the door would be locked, even though I knew it wasn't. I swallowed a lump in my throat before I could talk again.

"Brought men in to build the house. But the actual land was just a little plot, a few acres. Not enough room to raise anything there. I was just a little scrap at the time, but I remember my dad and the sheep herders who worked for him laughing about how that guy might as well have thrown his money down the outhouse hole."

The truth was, my dad and the boys use to call him *that foreigner,* but knowing that Mr. Kahl had been referred to as that, and worse, I left that part out. It wouldn't be many years later till America entered the Great War against Germany, when the loyalty and very standing as Americans for people with German names like Mr. Kahl would be questioned by too many in this country. I've long since stopped betting in favor of how much brains people have when they have hate in their hearts.

Turning the knob, Mr. Kahl pushed the door open, the hinges squealing with rusty metal rubbing on rusty metal. I caught my breath, feeling my blood pounding.

"Then what?" Mr. Kahl looked over his shoulder at me, his gray eyebrows raised with curiosity when I realized I had fallen into silence for a moment or two too long.

"Then he just… disappeared." I shrugged with my hands out stretched to either side. "I guess nobody really noticed when exactly, as he stayed to himself. Stories started springing up like they do. Some people thought that he made his money as an outlaw, and that he headed off into the sunset when he thought the law was onto him. Others figured he got murdered for his money, and that his killer was living it up somewhere. Then, um…, people started talking about the place being haunted," my voice dropping to a hush, despite myself.

"Didn't he have any people back in Hungary who claimed the property? Or even any relatives here in this country?"

I watched Mr Kahl stroll through the doorway, turning his head about slowly as he surveyed the first floor. "No, I'm pretty sure they didn't," I answered. "I suppose that's how it ended up on the market, again."

"You coming in, Joseph?"

I cleared my throat before speaking, "Yeah, I am," and nodded as I walked inside, hoping I sounded brave. *C'mon, I'm too old to believe in ghosts, anymore,* I told myself as I took in the dust covered drapes that were only able to keep half the light outside from shining through the broken windows, filled with dust motes drifting in the air. The shapes of tables, chairs, and a couch stood in the half light. A tall, wide shape stood against the wall, which I knew was the a mahogany china hutch with a glass door, and a black wood stove and ice box stood idle in between the cabinets lining the walls of the kitchen. Some sort of painting in a fancy frame was barely visible above the gaping mouth of the fireplace at the other end of the first floor. It had changed little since I had been here that first and last time as a boy. "I just didn't want to crowd you, Mr. Kahl," I mumbled lamely.

Assuring me there was no problem with that, he muttered more to himself, "Some nice furniture left here. I might save some money with that." He tried the gas lamps along the wall, and found they had long since ceased to illuminate the house. I don't think he expected anything else.

When Mr. Kahl suggested we check out the two remaining upper stories, I slowly trailed behind him up the stairs, telling myself there were no ghosts or monsters in broad daylight. I fought to ignore my pulse thumping in my ears as my growing dread seemed to speak in a voice all it's own: *I don't want to be here. I don't want to be here.*

The second floor was filled with open doors leading to mostly empty rooms. "I guess I'll have to furnish this floor, after all," Mr. Kahl told me, going from one room to the next, till we found one where almost every inch of wall was hidden behind shelves filled with more books than I ever saw in my life. Sunlight poured into the room across the hallway from a window I think I had busted years before, revealing a desk and an overstuffed chair behind it, long unattended by a reader.

Walking inside, Mr. Kahl remarked that the missing owner appeared to be an avid reader, as he randomly pulled one book then another out to flip through. "Unfortunately, I'll have to learn to read Latin, and what I reckon is Hungarian, if I'm going to enjoy any of this library." He frowned, disappointed as he put the last book he looked at back on it's shelf. "Well, let's have a look upstairs while we still have light."

As I followed up the stairs behind Mr. Kahl, memories of a blackish red puddle of blood oozing out from under the door to the master bedroom filled my head, just as new and real to me as it had been when I had first seen it ten years before. Purplish spots filled my vision as I climbed the staircase, as my head became so light that

I was certain I must have been floating up the steps. That might have been pleasant were it not for how my stomach swam so violently, that I was certain that my breakfast and the meager lunch I had shared with my boss before coming here, was going to spray from my mouth all over his back ahead of me.

You're safe with Mr. Kahl, I tried persuading myself as I stepped unsteadily onto the third floor, taking in an upstairs foyer furnished with a couple wicker chairs situated around a table, outside the master bedroom. *He's tough, he's fearless, after all.* Or, at the very least, I thought what ever was behind that bedroom doorway would latch it's claws on his face first, maybe giving me time to run for my horse, I'm ashamed to admit.

My eyes drifted to the floor at the foot of the door, expecting to see at least a dried pool of blood as Mr. Kahl walked over and tried the knob. There was nothing there. *Of course not*, I told myself. *That had been almost ten years ago*, as I realized flies and other varmints would have eaten it up a long time ago. Also gone was the burlap sack full of chains and cowbells that I had left there years before. Probably taken by some hobo or vagrant who had stopped there for a rest, sometime or other, I figured.

I took a deep breath and held it as Mr. Kahl pushed the door open, my heart thumping under my ribs… That was when only rays of the sun hit his face as he stepped inside, I released my breath with a sense of relief and followed him inside.

The bed was huge, taking up the middle of the room, and with an extravagantly carved headboard bearing images of castles, forests, and mountains beneath a rich finish that caught the sunlight streaming through the window. Blankets and sheets hung half way off the mattress onto the hardwood floor, and a nightstand and a desk laid overturned on the floor. But no ghosts. No ghouls.

"Do you think there was a fight here?" Mr. Kahl turned his head to me, asking as if I was more than just a twenty two year old who nobody took seriously as a grown man.

I shrugged. "This place has been used by tramps and hobos since it's been deserted. I'd have thought they'd have left the house in worse condition."

Pushing open the double doors made up of glass window frames, Mr. Kahl walked out to the balcony at the back of the house. I

followed him outside, feeling foolish with myself. I had only been a
twelve year old boy ten years ago. Who knows what I had really
seen or heard that night. The two of us leaned against the railing,
both silent as we took in the sun drifting toward the horizon to the
west of the rolling country green with sage brush and grass where it
wasn't broken by outcrops of rusty color rock jutting from the earth.
I felt a sense of peace that moment, as I was finally able to let go of
the last of my childhood that I had allowed to follow me into
manhood.

"What do you suppose that is?" Mr. Kahl pointed to a doorway
set in what appeared to be a mound of brick that was maybe a
hundred yards away.

"I remember seeing that since I was a kid. My friends and I had
even tried opening the door, with no luck," I said. "I always thought
it might be a cellar of some sort."

"Whatever it is is beyond my property line," he mused, before
suggesting we take a look at it, anyhow.

When we walked up to the brick knoll after leaving the house, we
saw how the bricks had been badly laid and mortared, as if built in a
hurry. The weather beaten, wooden door and it's frame somehow
looked thick and well made, despite the sloppy brick work. There
was no doorknob or handle. Mr. Kahl put his hand against the
greying wood and gave it a shove, only to find it solidly locked.

"Well, I guess nobody's getting in," he said with a shake of his
head. "Whoever owns this piece of land can deal with it."

On the walk back to the house, Mr. Kahl pointed at a tiny door
above the balcony on the third story. "Strange place to put a door to
an attic," he mused, shaking his head. "I don't recall seeing any
door upstairs for the space under the roof." I nodded in agreement,
then put the eccentric feature of the house to slip out of my head.

We rode back to the bunkhouse as the sun set behind us.

Chapter II

Back in the summer of1902, all anyone could talk about was Harry Tracy, highway robber, gunman, and Hole-in-the-Wall desperado who had busted out of the Oregon state pen with his pard, Dave Merrill, leaving a trail of dead men and armed robberies behind them. Tracy readily took credit for having killed three prison guards during the daylight escape, and weeks later, three lawmen here in Washington fell to his guns. Even his own partner in crime, Dave Merrill, who he learned only after the prison break had betrayed him to the law back in Portland, got gunned down by the now famed outlaw on the run. This had hardly been Tracy's first turn on the dance floor, as he had escaped from prison in Utah, filled a rancher with lead in Colorado, and committed several holdups there and in the Northwest a few years before he made the national papers. By the summer of 1902, bounty hunters and lawmen from all over the west had joined the hunt for the badman in the greatest manhunt in the country's history, while newspapers from coast to coast had reporters swarming in the Northwest's woods to wire back electrifying headlines for an excitement hungry America.

And then it happened. Tracy had crossed the Cascades instead of fleeing north to Canada as everyone expected, and was heading across eastern Washington. Some whose hospitality he had obtained by the barrel of a gun reported he told them he was on his way back to the outlaw hide out, the Hole-In-The-Wall country in Wyoming, where, in his own words, "I'll be a thief among thieves, and safe."

For most people around here, it had been the summer of Harry Tracy. It should have been for me, too. But instead, me and my friends had to talk to that drifter, whistling as he walked along the road that August afternoon.

"Do you think that's Tracy?" I remember eight year old Jimmy Burton whispering, his eyes round and his mouth open with both fright and anticipation as we watched the man with the long, black beard approach us. We were carrying our fishing poles over our shoulders, heading back to my pa's sheep camp after playing hooky from work to fish at a local stream, only to find it dried up in the summer heat.

"Don't be stupid," his older brother, Teddy, snapped at him as he slapped the side of Jimmy's head with a loud smack. "Tracy's just got a mustache."

"Ow!" Jimmy winced as his rubbed the side of his head beneath the red hair he shared with his brother.

"Hey, that looks like it hurts!" The drifter smiled with an expression that was playful but with an affected ireful tone as he neared us, his bindle hanging behind him off the broom handle he held over his shoulder. The man's huge beard covered the upper half of his plaid work shirt, and his face was sunburned beneath his bowler. A revolver was holstered at the belt about the waist of his threadbare checkered pants, and his work boots were scuffed. I remember how he smelled like dirt and sweat, like he hadn't bathed in at least a week. Nothing out of the ordinary for the harvest bums and bindle stiffs I've known.

"I didn't mean anything by it, mister, honest." Pointing an accusatory finger at his little brother, Teddy said, "He thought you were Harry Tracy!"

The drifter howled with laughter. "Now, that's a man you should be avoiding at all cost."

"I suppose so, sir," he mumbled, looking like a dog expecting to be hit with a rolled up newspaper. Those days, grown ups took it upon themselves to punish misbehaving youngsters, related to them or not.

"Not to worry; I'm just funnin' you," he jostled Teddy's shoulder with his free hand. "Being the oldest kid in my family, I had to keep my brothers in line with a quick slap when I was your age."

Looking about the empty, rolling country, he asked, "Say, anyone hiring around here? I haven't seen a 'stead all day, just sage brush and more sage brush."

"There are plenty of farms and ranches hiring bums," Jimmy piped up, his face beaming with a smile.

This time Teddy slapped his little brother's head even harder, making the eight year old wipe at his eyes as they teared up.

"Sorry he's disrespectful, sir, but my dad dropped him on his head when he was a baby," Teddy explained, ignoring Jimmy who was glaring resentfully at him.

It was my turn to talk, I figured, as I took a step forward. "We were just heading to my pa's sheep camp a few miles away, but I don't think he needs anymore hands. There's some homesteads and cattle outfits maybe thirty or forty miles from here, though." There was bad blood between sheep herders and the sod busters and cattle men who didn't take kindly to flocks of animals being herded across land they were fencing off. My pa took care to avoid them and any violence that might break out.

"Huh, that's a long ways away," the drifter mumbled with a furrowed brow, I think more to himself than to us. "Sounds like I'll be sleeping outside, again tonight."

"Well, there's an empty farm house down the road." The words just seemed to pop out of my mouth on their own. In fact, we had quickened our pace past the abandoned house three miles down the road on the way back to my pa's camp.

"Yeah, but it's haunted," Jimmy said, his voice sounding chilled.

"Aint no such thing as ghosts!" Teddy raised his hand to slap his brother again, even though I remembered him being as spooked as me and his brother were. Jimmy scrambled away, covering his head of red hair with his hands.

"Well, I don't put much stock in ghosts, either, so a house of any sort might as well be a grand hotel," the drifter chuckled. "I don't cotton to sheepherders, anyhow, so I reckon I'll try out one of the cattle outfits or other, tomorrow," he said offhandedly. With a wave, he set off past us.

As we walked in the opposite direction, I kept looking over my shoulder at the drifter who became smaller and smaller, till he vanished over a hill, his words sounded in my head: *I don't cotton to sheepherders.*

I knew men like my pa had been gunned down by cowboys, hired guns, and settlers for the kind of work they did. Biting anger was welling up in the back of my throat.

***

Looking back today, I should have just shrugged off what that drifter said disparagingly about sheep herders; there was prejudices back then in this new, open country, then there was prejudice. But I was twelve years old back then, and fresh in my mind were memories of how a lot of the other kids as well as adults around here used to think of me and my pa as trash, and that had made what he said unforgivable in my mind.

That evening after dinner, I sat by the campfire that threw flickering shadows across the faces beneath the brimmed hats of everyone else present sitting around the flames.

My pa, big and rough, who owned this outfit, unscrewed the top off of a bottle of whiskey after a hard day's work. I never knew my mother, making him the only parent I had. Lucky me.

Teddy and his brother Jimmy, who was petting one of the sheep dogs draped over his lap, droopy eyed from herding sheep for his humans all day, both sat near me. Their pa, who was my dad's foreman, sat across the fire from them, playing the mouth organ, his red hair burned brown under the sun.

Four other sheepherders hired from the Spokane Indian reservation, their dark features proud and sad, laughed as they spoke with a mixture of English and their own language. That sheepherders like my pa often hired such men made race hatred directed at them somehow even more justifiable to many in this part of the country, along with what they also did for a living.

The horizon to the west was aflame with dusk along the edges of the darkening hills, while outside the firelight, the sky above was already turning black and filled with stars. Out in the dark, my pa's herd baaed and bleated as they lived their unthinking sheep lives of eating clover before falling asleep. All of that went unnoticed by me, as I sat on the soft earth with my arms wrapped around my knees, glowering into the flames as I listened to that drifter's voice over and over in my head.

"Something wrong, boy?"

My pa's voice pulled me out of my thoughts. I stared dumbly at him.

"You got a pretty angry look on your face, there." He smiled and took another swallow from his whiskey bottle, his sleepy eyed expression on his weather beaten, unshaven face, looking mildly drunk. "You pissed you couldn't catch any fish when you snuck off today?" he teased.

"Yeah, I guess," I answered with a quiet voice. Low laughter of the adults rumbled around the campfire, before the men went back to talking among themselves.

"You certain?"

I nodded.

My pa regarded me for a moment longer, as if he seemingly wanted to say something to me, before he turned away to talk to a gray haired Indian in his employ, and passed him the bottle. Back then, most men didn't know how to act tenderly, I suppose. They still don't. I went back to gaze into the flames, my thoughts smoldering.

Teddy scooted across the ground to me. He first glanced about the faces of the grown men in the dancing light and saw they were all occupied with adult talk of drinking, gambling, and women, before he whispered: "Your ass still smarting from what that bum said, today?"

I didn't need to answer him as I stared, unblinking, into the firelight.

"Well, I got an idea to make him sorry," Teddy kept his voice quiet, a smirk on his pale, freckled face.

***

The half moon shined brightly in the starry sky, but the three of us had taken care to bring a lantern with us when we had sneaked out of camp after everyone had gone to sleep beneath their blankets, their brains numbed with my Pa's whiskey. The oil lamp raised in Teddy's hand cast the dirt road between rocky ground and sage brush on either side in an orange glow as we made our way, fearful that we would still trip and break a leg despite the burning oil light. The burlap sack filled with chains and bells that I carried was weighing heavily, despite having switched arms frequently, and which rattled on the long night time walk.

An owl hooted somewhere in the dark.

"I knew the ghosts would get us if we done this," Jimmy wept as he turned his head about this way and that in fright. "I want to go home," he wailed, "I want to go home!"

"Shut up," Teddy snarled a whisper at his brother, as if their pa would somehow be able to hear the three of us from miles away. "I didn't want to bring you along, but you begged and raised a stink. So shut your mouth or I'll slap you across your head, again!"

"It's only an owl," I consoled the eight year old in a gentle voice, and with a jostle to his thin shoulder. "Nothing's out here at night that isn't here during the day." Sniffling, that seemed to settle Jimmy's nerves. The truth was, that owl hoot had made me jump, too.

The plan that Teddy had had for making the drifter pay for his derogatory words for sheep men involved the very reputation of the house we had told him about earlier in the day. That was where we three would enter into the darkened house, moaning and groaning, and making a racket with the chains and cowbells I brought along in the bag.

"But what about that pistol he's got in his holster?" We had slunk away from everyone else around the fire for the summer air that was finally cooling down with the dark, when I had asked Teddy a few hours ago.

"Don't worry about it," he had assured me with an uninterested waive of his hand. "Other than shooting coyotes and rattle snakes, that bum's probably too yellow to draw on a man, let alone a spook!"

I had nodded, but felt much less certainty than my friend did. I knew men like that had had a reputation for resorting to theft if work wasn't to be found, and sometimes that happened at the point of a gun. But that hadn't mattered to me; at least not for all that long. What burned in my head and ached at the back of my throat had been my one wish to make that drifter pay for his words.

It hadn't taken much time to find the chains and bells in the saddle bags of a pack mule after everyone else had hit the hay. All the while Jimmy, who had been listening in to Teddy and me, pleaded to come along, his voice becoming louder and shriller, till Teddy finally threw his hands up and gave in for fear the adults might be awakened.

The deserted house came into view as we followed the road over the last of the rolling hills, a looming, dark shape in the moonlight. That was when I realized my friends weren't walking besides me anymore as I followed the dirt road downward. I turned to find Teddy and Jimmy rooted to the ground in the lantern light.

"Well," I asked, looking from one still face to the other, "aren't we going to give it to that bum?"

"We don't know if he's even sleeping in there." Teddy's voice had become quiet and without any of the bravado he had shown earlier. "Besides, it's getting cold," despite the fact that the lamp was throwing off heat.

"I just want to go home," Jimmy's voice cracked, close to tears, his fingertips digging into his brother's free arm through his shirt sleeve. Teddy shrugged him off.

Storming back to the top of the slope, I yelled at Teddy, "This was your Goddamn idea!" The sack heavy with chains and bells slammed against the side of my leg with each hurried step, but I paid it little attention.

Teddy opened his mouth like he was going to say something angry back to me, then shut it and just let his head hang in shame, unable to look me in the face. I realized he was as afraid as his little brother was.

"Fine," I snarled with an angry sigh. "Give me the Goddamn lantern."

Teddy extended the lantern to me, dumbly. I took hold of it's metal handle more abruptly than I had intended and almost dropped it, not expecting the heat I felt in my palm and clenched fingers, yelling, "Ow!"

"It's too dark," I heard Jimmy whine behind me as I walked to the house. "It's too dark!"

"Shut up," Teddy told him in the same low voice.

Aggravated, I ignored them both, my jaws clenched. *My friends, who needs them,* I thought, feeling betrayed as I approached the waiting front door, lantern in one hand, and a bag of ghost effects in the other. Looking back, my anger for my friends, who were just boys same as me then, as with my anger for that drifter, were the thoughts of a twelve year old who had yet to learn that people could be fallible, just because they were people.

Turning the knob, and giving the door a shove, I thought I would have jumped out of my skin when the *scree-e-e-e-ch* filled the night air, till I realized it was only the rusty hinges. My heart thudded in my ears.

Closing my eyes with relief, I scolded myself, *There aint no such things as ghosts, so quit being a baby,* before I stepped inside, the lantern lighting my way. The furniture I saw in the glow was the same I had seen years later with Mr. Kahl. As was the painting above the open mouth of the fireplace of a stern faced man with dark hair and complexion, dressed in a lavish suit coat and tie like a tycoon from back east. There was no sight of the drifter sleeping on the first floor, so I climbed the stairs, my unblinking eyes staring straight ahead into the blackness before me, just beyond the light. My legs shook with each stair step upward with the weight of the chains and bells in the burlap bag, as well as with the fright I pretended I wasn't feeling.

I crept about the second floor in the darkness, slowly opening each door to peer inside, the orange light casting shadows against the walls, and fearful that creaky hinges would betray me to the sheepherder hating drifter. There was nothing. I began to wonder if the house had spooked him after all, and that he had just continued on past. But there was still one more flight of stairs to the third floor. *Might as well take a look*, I told myself, before heading upstairs, as the fear I had felt seemed to let loose of me. Half of me wanted the house to be empty; half of me wanted the bum to be fast asleep, ready for me to awaken with a ghost show that would leave his long johns full of shit.

There was only one door on the top story, I saw in the lamp light. *Makes it that much easier for me*, I thought as I emerged at the top story, feeling the cheerfulness returning to me from earlier in the day, before we met up with that bum. That was when the lamp light reflected off of something from the bottom of the bedroom door. I stared at the puddle, telling myself that it wasn't really blood. But growing up in the open country of the Northwest, I had seen plenty of animals slaughtered already in my time, and I knew just what that pool was.

My stomach dropped, and fear's chilly fingers crawled up my spine. Faintly, I could hear a sound on the other side of the door. It was wet… slurping.

A voice in my head was screaming for me to go, even as my hand reached out and turned the handle, and pushed the door open, while holding the lantern away, so as not to awaken the man. I peered in the narrow space from the door and it's frame, the moon shining brightly through the open window at the back of the room, seeing the stick thin, skeletal thing hunched over the sprawled body on the bed. It's face was beneath the drifter's thick, black beard, shaking his body roughly on the mattress, feeding ravenously as would a dog with a rabbit in it's jaws. The tell tale blood smeared between the bed and the door was black in the dim light. He had tried to reach the door and get away, I realized.

The thing looked up from it's meal at me, it's face hidden in the darkness from the moonlight behind it. Eyes wide with stark terror, I felt my bladder fill as I slammed the door shut. Dropping the bag as I ran for the stairs, I heard the chains and cowbells inside clatter noisily on the wooden floorboards. The lantern swinging in my hand as I took the steps two or three at a time, I glanced back before the third floor disappeared from view, when I saw the bedroom door opening.

I burst out of the house, throwing the front door wide open, my heart pounding so hard and fast I was certain it would explode in my chest as I ran faster than I had ever before into the blackness.

"Hey, what's…," I heard Teddy's familiar voice in front of me, when I ran right into him, the two of us tumbling hard to the ground. I felt my bladder empty, piss soaking the front of my pants. The lantern flew from my hand, flames flaring out of the broken glass where it shattered on the road.

"Run!" I was up from the ground instantly, pulling my stunned friend to his feet, and yelled at him and his brother, "For God's sakes, run!"

Both Teddy and Jimmy later told me that it was the look of a madman on my face that made them turn and race into the darkness with me.

***

Even eight years later, I can still recall how my pa gave me the whippin' of my life the next day, despite being twelve, already.

He whipped me for losing expensive equipment like the lantern, and those chains and cowbells. I had lied and told him I had just dropped the last off on the road, fearing he would have made me go back to the house to get them. "D'yuh think I'm made of money, boy?" he had roared at me with each strike of his belt on my backside, *WHACK, WHACK,* after he had wrestled me to the ground and pulled my jeans and long johns down to my knees.

He whipped me for sneaking out at night, thoughtless of the chance that I could have gotten my friends and me killed by rattle snakes slithering in the dark.

But especially, I think, he whipped me because of the insanely unbelievable story I had told him in a breathless whisper of the thing that had killed the drifter.

Soon afterward, word came that Tracy was dead and that his body was being displayed in the nearby town of Davenport for all to see. Our fathers took time off of work to take Teddy, Jimmy, and me to see the desperado's corpse. Word was, Tracy had been hiding out on a ranch when a young cowboy who had led him there informed on him. In the ensuing gun battle with a local posse, the most feared badman of his time got shot up and was trapped in a nearby wheatfield. With no hope of escape, Tracy had put his six gun above his right eye and pulled the trigger. The next morning, only a couple of the posse men had the courage to walk into the field, where they discovered the body.

The doctor's office was crowded as everyone tried to get a glimpse of the emaciated body dressed in blood drenched clothing, layed out on a cot. I recall seeing the grisly, self inflicted crater where Tracy's eye should have been, and his big hands folded on his torso, just briefly between jostling onlookers. When the citizens began ripping off shreds of dirty, blood splattered clothing, and snipping hair off the dead outlaw's head, the doctor roared at everyone to get out.

It was only when we were outside that I realized my heart was pounding in my chest. I was quiet for the rest of that day – and onward – while my two friends could talk of nothing but Tracy's body.
That night, I awakened with a girlish shrill after a nightmare of being in the doctor's office, when Tracy's body sat up and turned his shattered head to me face me. And then it wasn't Harry Tracy anymore, but the shadowed, skeletal thing I had seen in that house.

After that for the next following years, I had had the reputation of being a liar with an overactive imagination. Not that it mattered, as I ended up withdrawing from everyone else around me, spending time with my lonesome watching the sheep while on the job with my pa. That is till darkness fell, and I wouldn't say outside any longer. Most nights I'd wake up, screaming. I sometimes still do. The brash kid with the fly away smile, who had always been ready to skip out of work to go fishing or just get into trouble, had seemingly departed, leaving this silent, haunted eyed sleepwalker I had become in his place.

Teddy and Jimmy never talked about what I told them I had seen that night. In fact, they seemed content to just assume I had made the whole thing up, and eventually just stopped having anything to do with me at all. I remember their smirks when they'd eye me and whisper into the ears of our schoolmates about how there was something wrong with me, and how it was best to stay away. Everyone got to talking about me as being wrong in the head, whether I was in earshot or not. *My friends.* I suppose I can't blame them entirely. Before that night, I'd have whipped any other kid who'd call me those things, but after, I shied away from fisticuffs, and just went off to be alone. Like I said, the boy named Joe who snuck into that house that night wasn't the same as the one who came running out.

When I was fifteen, Teddy and Jimmy left with their pa for work in Montana. I'm sure if things had been different, if I hadn't gone to that house that night, I would have cried like a baby for losing my two best friends. But I had, and so I could have cared less if they were gone for deserting me. I later heard the two brothers had fallen in with bad company, and had tried robbing a diner when Teddy had been shot dead by the shotgun wielding proprietor. A wounded Jimmy was captured days later and sentenced to prison by the testimony of the hardcase who had talked them into the holdup in the first place.

Two years ago, my pa died of a stroke after someone had poisoned our sheep, and we had lost the house after the money stopped coming in. I always thought it was an Irish farmer who had taken offense when our sheep had strayed into his cornfield, but there's no way I could prove it. I didn't have any interest in taking up my emotionally distant pa's line of work, as he had seemed to think I was just a loss, anyway. So instead I went from stead to stead, finding work as a hired hand where I could. And that's how I eventually went to work for Mr. Kahl, the generous, gregarious man who was the best boss I ever had, and who I wished could have been my father.

Chapter III

Any fear I had remaining for that house seemed to disappear when Mr. Kahl had me work with him taking care of the disrepair, and throwing out the furniture that had either gotten colonized by mice, or had attracted mold. Mr. Kahl hired an electrician from Spokane to put in electric wiring and light fixtures, after he and I ripped out all the gas fittings. The rest of the hands were told to plant wheat, and take care of the livestock. Oh, the other boys had their fun in the second, newly built bunk house after dusk, calling me the golden boy and the boss' favorite. But there was no malice in it, with the exception of McMurty from time-to-time, and I rather appreciated being treated like someone special for once in my life.

Then the animals started showing up dead.

The hands working the fields would find rabbits or marmots dead, their throats torn out, if their heads hadn't been ripped off entirely.

Flies would buzz over the tiny corpses already stinking amid the dry grass and brush in the spring air. Coyotes were the explanation, and so no one payed it much mind, as long as Mr. Kahl's animals were left alone.

But then one morning, in the coop where the chickens had been moved to nearer to the house, dead birds were scattered behind the wire fence we had put up, lying about the ground, wings splayed about. Bodies of chickens were torn open and often headless, dried blood turned dark plastering their feathered bodies. Those chickens that remained inside the small building made of unpainted boards had also been torn apart, the straw where the hens had made their nests painted black-red with drying blood and innards.

Mr. Kahl shook his head, a furious look on his bearded face. He cursed in German, which I had already come to learn meant: *Goddamn son-of-a-bitch!* Grabbing at his hat, he slapped it against his thigh as he eyed the hole dug under the chicken wire, livid with rage.

"Well, I guess we aint gonna have eggs for a while," Charlie McMurty, the hand who had pounded on the house' door that morning to tell Mr. Kahl about the dead fowl, guffawed with a wide mouthed smile, his thumbs hooked on the straps of his overalls.

Mr. Kahl gave him a hard stare, as to tell McMurty that his jovial quip hadn't been appreciated. McMurty shied away, his eyes down at his feet shifting about uncomfortably. "Well, did anyone see any wild animals around the property? Did anyone hear anything?" Mr. Kahl looked at all of us who had gathered around the chicken coop. All of us could only shake our heads no. "Well, Charlie, if you're missing eggs so much, you can patrol the property with a rifle to kill any filthy predators you can find," Mr. Kahl snapped at McMurty. "Apparently, Joseph and I have to go to town to buy more birds."

***

It was in early summer that Josephine Kahl arrived on the train from South Dakota. Mr. Kahl had left for Davenport to pick her up in his buckboard wagon, while I finished painting the interior walls of the house. I was walking from the house to the water pump to wash up when I saw her, strolling alongside her father on the pathway toward the house, chatting in German as they both smiled and laughed. Her flower patterned dress swished about her long legs as she stepped cautiously about the rocky, uneven ground in her dusty, leather shoes.

Turning to me with a grin as soon as he saw me, Mr. Kahl said, "Josie, this is my hardest working, most loyal hired man, Joseph MacReady," giving me a reverent bow. I could feel my face reddening as I tried not to look too stupid as I smiled back. "And this, Joseph, is the light of my life, my daughter, Josephine Kahl."

"My father speaks well of you," she said, her voice easily transitioning from the German accent of her father to sounding like any American woman I've ever had the pleasure of making the acquaintance this far west. She extended a hand to me with a gentle grin. I awkwardly took her hand, already feeling clumsy and ill at ease with myself. The hand I took was soft, making me all the more self conscious of my own calloused paws, and my paint stained work clothes.

She was her father's daughter in that she was tall and long faced. But while his features were weathered and creased with age, hers were soft and fair with youth. Her light brown hair was pinned and combed behind her head, fluttering in the light breeze. Realizing I had been staring at her for a moment or two longer than I had intended, I let loose of her hand with a timid laugh.

"Oh," she gasped as she looked at the paint splotching her fingers and palms. She put her other hand up to the smile on her mouth.

I mumbled, "I'll show you where the water pump is," my face growing even redder as Mr. Kahl howled with laughter.

I quietly left as Mr. Kahl pumped the handle for the water as Josie held her hands spilling from the spigot while vigorously scrubbing the still wet paint off with the other. Figuring that I could wash my hands later, I searched for more work to do in the house. Anything to hide from the eyes of others, and the sense of discomfiture that came with it; a feeling only understood by other social outcasts.

It wasn't that I had never been with a woman. When payday came, I'd be hitting the red light district in any one of the surrounding towns with the other hands, getting rid of that itch I felt below my belt with which ever sporting lady was free to open her

legs for money. But there had never been a sweetheart in my life as
with the boys who I had grown up with had. The two or three barn
dances I had gathered my courage up to attend left me all the more
dejected as every girl there turned me down when I had asked them
to dance. I remember the sideways glances at me as I had stood by
the barn door, hat in hand and eyes close to tearing as dance partners
whirled past me. Every so often, I would catch the cruel smiles as
words were whispered into someone else' ear. I was still the guy
who wasn't right in the head, ever since that night when I was twelve
years old.

There was no reason for me to believe the stunning girl with the
good nature I had met that day was going to see me any differently.

Chapter IV

The sound of our hammers pounding nails inside the barn echoed
in the morning air as Mr. Kahl and I put up a railing in the loft
above, when from the open window across from us, we both heard
Juliani's panicked voice from outside.

"Boss! Something's killed one of the cows! Santa Maria!"

I followed behind Mr. Kahl as he scurried half way down the
wood ladder till he leaped the rest of the way down to the barn floor.
Knees buckling, he fell but caught himself with arms out and hands
splayed on the dirt floor. Juliani, who had just raced inside the barn,
and I helped the boss to his feet.

"What the hell are you talking about?" Mr. Kahl absently brushed his dirtied hands off on his faded overalls, and demanded, "Was it an animal attack?"

His brown eyes wide in his normally dark face now paling, Juliani gasped for breath from running as he spoke: "We found one of the heifers laying on it's side out in the pasture. Her throat was ripped out!"

"Show me," Mr Kahl demanded, even though he rushed out of the barn first, leading the way.

It hadn't taken long for the three of us to find the cow lying on her side in the grassy pasture, a mound of white and brown fur that the other cattle grazed mindlessly about. Her eyes stared blankly and her blackened, shriveled tongue hung from her bloody mouth, curled on the ground. But it was the gruesome hole ripped into the side of her neck, caked with dried blood that was still not enough to hide the exposed, blackish-red vertebra deep within that drew all our attention. Crouching down, Mr. Kahl scowled as he examined the wound where flies already buzzed about, landing to feed or lay eggs. Juliani crossed himself and muttered what I took to be a prayer in Italian or Latin.

I took a few steps behind Mr. Kahl to look over his shoulder, and the memory of the skeleton thin thing feeding on the throat of the harvest bum from eight years before flashed through my mind. Putting the thought from my mind, I cleared my throat in order to steady my voice before I spoke. "Think it was coyotes?"

"Had to be," Mr. Kahl sighed with disgust, before he took back to his feet. "Where the hell is McMurty?" He looked about the pasture, and at the house and out buildings in the distance. "He was supposed to have taken care of all this."

"He's working the wheat field with Cranston, today," Juliani answered, still looking white as a ghost. "I'll go get him."

Shaking his head, Mr. Kahl snapped, "No, *I'll* get him." As he stormed off, he looked over his shoulder and told me, "I'll be back to help you in the barn as soon as I can."

Good for his word, Mr. Kahl came back to the barn and helped me finish the carpentry work. His normally jovial mood having given way to a morose silence, I didn't ask him what had happened out in the fields between him and McMurty as I continued to nail boards into place.

I found out about the words the two had had from the boys later on when we went back to the house for lunch. I had sat down at the kitchen table, thanking Josie for the ham sandwich and a stein of beer she had placed before me on a chipped porcelain plate, when Cranston pulled back the chair beside me and took a seat.

"You might want to keep out of McMurty's way," he mumbled to me just above a whisper.

"How's that?" I stared questioningly at the raw boned face with graying whiskers around the chin. "What did I do?"

"Nothing," Gary said with a shake of his head as he took another seat. "But did that ever stop that asshole from cutting someone down?" Both he and Cranston fell quiet as Josie returned from making up two more sandwiches on the cutting board on the other side of the kitchen. They both thanked her kindly when she left, then returned with two more mugs of beer. Walking away, she gave me a knowing glance. Of course she could hear the conversation that was supposed to be only between the men. I smiled weakly back at her. Truth was, Josie I had found out was a woman of some education, and who was in fact looking over the paperwork she could read in the house' library in order to find any possible relative of the former owner to avoid future possible legal entanglements when she wasn't cooking. Juliani came in and said a prayer over the food Josie brought him.

Cranston took a swig of beer before speaking, his voice low.

"Well, the boss storms up to the horses pulling the combine McMurty was driving, and grabbed hold of the bridle of the one at the front to make it stop. And did he ever bitch McMurty out! The boss wanted to know just what the hell he was doing when he was supposed to be riding around looking for coyotes, wolves, or anything else that might've kill the animals. McMurty started yelling back that he had killed five coyotes on and around the property, and that he had looked damn hard for them over the week he had set out on horseback."

And that was true, I recalled… to an extent. McMurty had come back with *a* dead coyote to show off to the rest of us with that overbearing grin of his, but hardly five of them. In fact, one of the other wheat farmers around here mentioned how Mr. Kahl's man was spending most of his time loitering around saloons in Odessa and Reardan, getting drunk. Mr. Kahl had just shook his head, clamped his jaws tight, and breathed out what sounded like steam from his long, crooked nose. Any other boss would have fired McMurty for that. But Mr. Kahl would be more likely to shoot himself in the foot than to fire a man well into the season and leave him without a means of survival. Oh, he let it go, but that steam was building up inside all that time till now.

But I'm straying from the subject. Cranston continued: "Boss told him he had it under good information that he had been seen at local drinking establishments, looking for coyotes and wolves at the bottom of a whiskey glass instead of riding the range. He told McMurty he was lucky he wasn't fired for being lazy drunk and a liar, and that any other man working for him could have done a better job with a rifle to clear varmints from the property. That's when McMurty had to go and talk back to him with: "I suppose meaning that foggy brained golden boy of yours, who...'"

Cranston fell silent when McMurty swung the front door open hard enough to rattle loundly against the wall behind. Slamming the door shut behind him, McMurty walked to the kitchen table with his head down, and his pinched face smoldering. I saw his swollen, black eye, as I know everyone else at the table had, too, before I just looked away and chewed my food in silence. Garry and Cranston began chuckling under their breath while casting furtive, knowing glances at the big cowboy.

That was when I felt the meaty palm of McMurty's hand slap me hard across the side of my head. "Laugh at me, you crazy little shit," I heard his voice through the pain and stunned ringing in my head as the kitchen tipped to the side. The hardwood floor was jarring as I hit it shoulder first, accompanied by the clatter of the overturned chair.

"Jesus, McMurty! He didn't do anything," I heard Cranston yell. His chair's legs screeched against the floor as he stood up.

"Mind your own business, you Goddaamn hobo," McMurty yelled back.

I started to push myself up with one hand while I held the other against the smarting pain on the side of my head, when McMurty buried the tip of his boot into my stomach, making me collapse back to the floor, the pain making me wretch breathlessly as I fought to keep my lunch down. Tears welled up through my tightly squeezed eyes lids.

"Leave him alone!" It was Josie's voice shrill with anger and alarm. "Leave him alone, or my father will have your hide!"

McMurty's laugh above me was cruel and without humor. "Oh, I'm sure your daddy's gonna stick up for his golden boy. Christ knows this sack of shit on the floor doesn't have the balls to stick up for himself."

I'm not sure exactly why I did what I did next, save to say that the rage inside made my sight red as I pushed myself up from the floor again, and with all my might threw my fist into the crotch of McMurty's pants. McMurty made a high, whining cry as he fell to the floor's hardwood boards in front of me, clutching his privates, his face dead white and his one unblackened eye bulging. Then I was on top of him, my teeth bared with all the rage I had kept pushed down deep inside. I struck at the unshaven face again and again, which disappeared in a splatter of blood as his nose broke and his lips were mashed against shattering teeth beneath my fists. Voices called my name as I felt hands trying to pull me off of him, but I just ignored them.

"Joseph, stop, this very instant! Do you hear me?" It was Mr. Kahl's German accented voice that made the reddish fog clear from my sight, and my blows slow to a stop. "I'm not having any brawling in my house!" I hadn't even realized he had come inside.

"Dad, Joe was only defending himself," Josie said as she put her hands on my side and beneath my armpit to help me stand back up.

"That's right, boss," Gary added, pushing back his chair to stand up from the table. "He attacked Joe out of the blue." Cranston and Juliani both nodded, adding that it had all apparently happened because McMurty was sore over the raking-over-the-coals the boss had given him, and took it out on Joe.

My head swimming as my body trembled, I swayed on my feet as I looked at my bloody hands, then at the cow puncher on the floor, his breathing quaking between having to cough and gag on his own blood. He held up a hand, palm up and fingers splayed, for mercy as he was in no condition to speak. I shuddered, but my heart raced, too. It had been as if the past eight years had been revoked, and I could be that happy kid who never backed down from a fight, again. All it took, apparently, was having the shit kicked out of me.

Nodding, Mr. Kahl regarded McMurty, who was attempting to sit up. "Alright, help him to his feet before he drowns on his own blood. Clean him up, then tell me and I'll give him his pay. Then he's free to find new employment."

"Please, no," I said as I offered my hand to the man who had just attacked me out of his petty pride and envy. With a moment's hesitation, McMurty took my hand, and I pulled him up, though he swayed unsteadily and had to grab for the edge of the table before he fell. "I don't want to cost a man his livelihood just over a fight." I touched the side of my head, feeling it growing hot and swollen.

Mr. Kahl just sighed with a bewildered look, and shook his head. "Alright, get him cleaned up," he told the other hired men.

Putting an arm around either side of the big cowboy, Gary and Cranston pulled him along, grunting with exertion for the man's weight. His head lolled about as he seemed to drift in and out of consciousness while the two steered him around to take him outside, his feet half dragging as he tried to walk. Juliani rushed ahead to open the door for the men, when I saw McMurty glance over his shoulder at me. Beneath the swelling and blood, I think he appeared as bewildered as Mr. Kahl did.

"Some dumb luck to get your ass kicked twice in the same day," Mr. Kahl wisecracked loud enough for McMurty to hear as he watched the three leave the house. Turning to face me, he asked, "Are you alright, Joseph? It looks like that handprint on the side of your head is going to turn into a bruise."

Keeping my eyes down to the floor, I muttered, "I'm okay, but I'm sorry for all that, Mr. Kahl," hearing how small my voice was with genuine shame for fighting in his house. But more, I became acutely aware that Josie still had an arm around my shoulder – the shoulder of just a hired hand – in front of her father.

Mr. Kahl shook his head. "I never much liked that asshole, anyway. If you change your mind, he's gone." I thanked him, but said I didn't think that would be necessary.

"I'll get him a steak to put on that," Josie said kindly with a smile, as she noticed how my own fingers gingerly touched the swelling mark McMurty left on the side of my head.

***

I was in the barn, pitching hay for the horses, when McMurty strolled through the doorway. I kept my eyes away from him, my manner cold and emotionless. Head down and thumbs through his pant's belt loops, he stayed silent for several moments, before saying conversationally, "Long day. Glad it's almost over." And that was true as the light outside the barn door was cast in the dimming light of the setting sun, making shadows long and dark in the mid summer evening.

"I suppose so." I gripped the pitchfork's shaft, half expecting a fist to be thrown at me.

After another moment's silence, he looked up at me. "Why did you stick up for me? I wouldn't have."

I turned to face him, seeing how his face was still puffy, and his nose now crooked to the right side from our fight a couple days before, despite the growing shadows. But the cruel humor and arrogance was gone, I saw. Lowering the iron prongs of the pitchfork to the dirt floor, I said, "Because I know what it's like to be the odd man out, and without a friend in sight."

Chapter V

"Joe!"

I turned my head at the sound of Josie's voice as I was heading to the cow pasture. She walked from the front door of the house, her smile and her eyes radiant. I saw her long legs silhouetted through her light blue dress in the morning light, and felt my heart pick up a beat. I looked away, feeling as if I had overstepped my bounds, and muttered, "Morning, Miss Kahl."

"Oh, dispense with that silly *Miss Kahl* stuff," she laughed as she stepped up to me. "I'm Josie. Everyone else calls me by my name."

The truth was, while every other hired man had been calling her by her first name, she remained Miss Kahl to me. I just grunted with a shrug of my shoulders.

"Are you blushing? I'm sorry if I make you feel uncomfortable," she said with a frown. "I can leave you alone if..."

"No... no, please," I spoke up with maybe too much enthusiasm, then followed that with an awkward chuckle. "I... I just... Your dad wants me to put up some more barbed wire," I stammered, not really sure what to say as I looked down at my work boots and absently rubbed the back of my neck.

"Yes, I know," she said, nodding with a smile, and clutching her hands together at her waist. "I asked him if I could get you to do another job for me."

"Sure, of course!" Again, I thought I was sounding too eager to please.

"You probably heard my dad had me going through Victor Nagy's papers."

"I'm sorry... who?" I shook my head.

"The previous owner, who built this house."

"Oh, of course." In all my years, I never knew the name of the man who had owned this property, save by the monikers, the *Hungarian,* or the *foreigner.* It was the first time I had a name to put to the faceless man who had inspired so many ghost stories by vanishing.

"As I said, I was going over the paperwork we found inside the desk in the library... what paperwork that was in English or German. Anyhow, I found the name and address of an apparent relative living in Seattle. So my dad wrote a letter to this relative of Mr. Nagy's, explaining how he bought the property, and hoped any legal matters about ownership could be avoided. Well, my dad would normally accompany me to Davenport post office, but he has his hands full, so he suggested I ask you to come with me. He said you were the best gentleman he knew."

She smiled sweetly. I figured, *Why not.*

***

The country of sage brush, grass, and broken rock stretched out monotonously as far as the eye could see in front of us, as Josie and I rode together in the buckboard wagon, the reigns in my hands for the horses that pulled us leisurely along down the dirt road. It was a warm, mid summer day, and I had a lovely woman as my companion who seemed to enjoy chatting with me, so I had no real complaints. Occassionally, she took her wide brimmed hat off with a feigned look of irritation, and swatted a bug flying too close. The leather case where Mr. Kahl's inquiries to Nagy's relation on the other side of the Cascades, as well as other mail, sat on the wagon floor between her feet.

Josie had talked about about how impressed she was with me for going so easy on McMurty, when she said out of the blue, "This is the most I've heard you ever say, I think." She turned her face to me with that smile, again. "Not that that's a bad thing," she hurriedly added. "I've known too many men who babble without sense, non-stop." She giggled.

"I don't talk a lot to most people," I muttered, keeping my eyes straight ahead. "Most people don't take to me, I guess," I added a few moments later. A black cloud inside me threatened to dampen the bright sky above.

"Why is that?" she asked kindly.

"People around here… call me foggy headed, a liar, and worse."

Folding her hands on her lap, she took a deep breath before speaking. "Let me begin with saying, my dad let me in what an exceptional young man you are, despite a reputation folks around here saddled you with." Looking back at me, she smiled again. "And seeing the kind of man you are, I concur."

Thanking her, we rode on in silence, till I finally said: "The things they say about me… about what I thought I saw in that house… your house, when I was twelve, and how I might as well have been a sleep walker for the rest of my growing up… that's all true." I felt my mouth go dry, despairing I may have lost another friend with needing to tell the truth. Her gentle hand on my knee took me by surprise.

"What did you see?" she asked softly.

Hesitantly at first, I recalled the story of the angry twelve year old I had been. Of how me and my two friends decided to scare the bowels loose of the harvest bum who had made a disparaging remark about sheep men like our fathers, by putting on a spook show in the empty house reputed to be haunted. By the time I was describing the skeleton thin thing feeding on the tramp, I had broken out into a sweat, and my hoarse voice was trembling, even after all these years.

Josie had remained quiet for the entire time I told her the story, her face unexpressive but thoughtful at the same time. When she did speak, her voice was low. "My mutti used to keep me awake all night as a girl, with her stories about ghosts and worse. She said some of those stories were even true, and she never steered me wrong." Shrugging her shoulders, she continued, "My dad hardly believes in anything he can't see or touch, but my mutti was different." Memories seemed to be coming to life behind Josie's eyes, giving her a far away look as she spoke to me. "She thought there were things in this world that were unseen unless they wanted to be, and those things usually meant none of us any good." Then, with a blink of her eyes and a shake of her head, she was back. "So, yes, I do believe you." She nodded slowly. "I believe you saw… something that frightened you as a boy. Whatever it was, I think it's gone now," she told me, hoping to sound convincing to me. Maybe to herself, as well.

Again, we both were silent as we rode on. I didn't know if the conversation had unnerved her as it had me. Thoughts about what to talk about next whirled about in my head, till I allowed myself to blurt one of those out. "Where is your mom… your mutti, now?"

She glanced down at her hands folded on her lap with a sad look. "She died five years ago."

"Oh, I'm sorry… I shouldn't have..."

"No, no, it's alright." She gently waved me off. "We had a dry, dry summer that year in South Dakota. My dad had been branding horses that day. He said afterward he couldn't remember if he had extinguished the branding iron in a bucket of water, or not. It was the horses screaming that woke me up that night. I ran outside to see the barn ablaze, and my mutti in her night shift running into the barn door to save the animals." She fell silent for a moment, recalling the bad memories I understood would still hurt, even after five years.

"It's alright." It was my turn to be consoling, as I touched her hand. She didn't jerk it away from me, as I was half afraid she would.

"My dad ran after her, and yelled at her to stop, to come back. He knew there wasn't any hope for the horses, but she rushed inside. And then the whole structure collapsed. We found her in the morning. She had actually gotten a stall open before she died. My dad..." She stopped to clear her throat. "My dad couldn't forgive himself. He was so certain he must not have taken care of that branding iron, even though I told him it didn't matter. It was all an accident. After that, he did what men always seemed to do after losing the love of their lives, and tried drinking himself to death, while he let the farm go. Every night, I could hear him crying in his bedroom. At one time, he even talked about going back to the Crimea in Russia out of homesickness. Even though he had told me how, when he was young, he and his family had fled from there for fear of lynch mobs, or… progroms, as the Russians called them."

"I didn't know any of that," I confessed. It was almost impossible for me to picture Mr. Kahl in such a hopeless state of mind. "Is that why he came here?"

"It was." She nodded. "It was obvious everywhere he looked in our old place, he saw mutti, and that he couldn't get any better staying there. So I told him how a lot of other Russian Germans were moving to the states in the Northwest, and eventually talked him into coming here."

Feeling the words straining to get past my lips, after a pause I said, "Well, I'm glad you both came here." Feeling a blush coming on for just saying something as simple as that, I looked away and gave the reigns a little snap.

"Thank you. I'm glad we came here, too." She leaned her shoulder against mine.

She made my heart soar.

***

Davenport was hardly a thriving metropolis by any means, but it had the amenities – saloons, a red light district, stores, a railroad depot, and a post office. Leaving the horses and our wagon at the livery stable, Josie and I walked down the mainstreet – which was a wide dirt road with the town's businesses on either side – to deliver the mail, including Mr. Kahl's letter. Townsfolk, as well as farmers, ranchers, sheepmen, and their hands from the steads in the surrounding countryside milled about us, going about their business on foot, horseback, or wagon. I nodded to familiar faces passing by. And yet, powerlines had already been strung up between towering wooden poles, bringing electricity and even phone service to what otherwise might have been a frontier town a decade or two before.

At the post office, a couple men sitting on the outside steps turned their heads to watch us approach with narrowed eyes. One, who wore a straw hat and overalls, set his harmonica he had been playing down on his lap. The other, whose flannel shirt was rolled up at the sleeves, tipped his cowboy hat to Josie with a smile I somehow found unsettling, as his eyes fixed on her bag. Both were in need of a shave and a bath. As we passed by them to enter through the front door, which jingled with a bell, I couldn't help but see the bulge of a revolver inside the harmonica player's overalls, near his waist.

"Hello! Hello!" called the postal clerk behind the counter. He was a small man with a huge, graying mustache, dressed in a striped shirt. The office itself was much smaller than I would have expected. "Got mail to pick up, or going out?"

"Going out," Josie answered, setting her bag on the counter to remove the letters.

Ringing up the postage on the cash register, the clerk announced, "That'll be five cents."

As Joise payed the man from an inner pocket inside the bag, I glowered while thinking five cents was no better than highway robbery.

Walking out, I let her know my opinon about the postage stamp racket, to which she couldn't help but laugh. "It's okay, Joe. The government has to make money somehow to keep the mail going to where ever.”

Neither of us took notice of how the two men on the steps outside were gone.

***

“I’m famished,” Joise said as we walked back down the mainstreet. “Can you suggest somewhere good to eat?”

“Um…, I usually just get food at one of the saloons whenever I’m in town,” I offered lamely, readjusting my hat awkwardly at my absurd suggestion. Then added quickly, “But I’m sure we can find something else, though.” The truth was, women were a rarity in saloons, save for the kind who were accused of being of a certain reputation. Or so I had been raised to believe.

She smiled at me humorously with a furrowed brow, as if she knew what I was thinking. “Back in South Dakota when I was growing up, I used to accompany my dad to the saloon for something to eat from time to time,” she spoke as we walked. “I suppose because I was an only child, and I wasn’t a boy...”

She fell silent at the sound of a revolver cocking from the alleyway we were just walking past. “Hand over that bag, and stay quiet.” The man dressed in overalls and straw hat held the six gun at eye level from the shade cast between the two buildings.

“Don’t even think about calling for help,” growled the other man in the cowboy hat from behind his friend, holding out his empty hands for her bag. I immediately thought there was only one gun between the two of them. There were passerbys on the street, but none close enough to risk calling for help.

Josie’s eyes went fearfully from one hold-up man to the other, then to me, before saying, “Please, just let me give you the money I’ve got in the bag. It was a gift from my mutti, and...”

“You’re what?” demanded the one with the gun.

“Her mother,” I muttered.

She nodded her head. “She died five years ago, and this is the only thing I have to remember her by,” she said, biting her lip and blinking her eyes as if she was about to tear up.

"Shit, keep the Goddamn thing! Just hold over the money." He motioned to the leather bag in her hand.

"Thank you! Thank you!" Josie laughed with relief as she undid the brass snap with one hand, and reached inside with the other. She let the bag fall to the ground as she pulled a six shooter out and aimed it at the robber with the gun. Her expression turned hard. "Alright, put the gun away, or we can see which of us is quicker on the trigger." It was her turn to pull back the hammer with a click.

Admittedly, I only stared with my damn fool mouth open, just as taken by surprise as the two would-be-robbers were.

The man in the cowboy hat first backed away with his hands raised in the air and with a fearful look on his face, before he whirled around and ran away down the alley, his feet thumping loudly.

The man wearing the straw hat turned to look behind him at his fleeing friend, muttering with disgust, "Of all the lily livered..." That was when I acted, grabbing hold of his outstretched wrist to wrench his gun pointed at Josie away, when I threw a fist at his face. The would-be-robber dropped to the ground at the alley's mouth, his finger pulling the trigger again and again, with a *click... click... click.*

"The damn thing aint even loaded," I said with amazement to Josie with a shake of my head. The gunman laid at our feet, eyes dazed, and his straw hat having fallen off of his balding head. First picking up her bag to put her gun back, Josie turned to call for help with a wave of her hand to the locals walking by

"Didn't want to hurt anyone, just got no money," the disarmed robber said, his voice woozy as he tried sitting up, only to fall back to the ground, still stunned by my love tap. The buise on the side of his jaw already looked as if would grow into a goose egg.

***

As it turned out, Josie and I ended up waiting to press charges at the Davenport Sheriff's office for the next few hours, as the sheriff had been about county business that day. The man who had tried robbing us had been locked into a cell by concerned citizens, where he sat on the bottom bunk pressing a hand against his swelling jaw. The top bunk was occupied by a disheveled man who snored loudly, one arm hanging off his mattress. We were told that was the town drunk, who was always getting thrown into the clinker. Someone even brought us something to eat from one of the saloons when Josie said she was starving. As I listened to Josie engage me in small talk, I folded my arms over my chest, and tipped my head, feeling just a tad bit tired…

"Joe." I heard Josie's soft voice in the darkness of sleep. Her hand lightly jostled me by my shoulder to wakefulness. "The sheriff's back."

Blinking sleep from my eyes as I raised my head, I saw the street lights were on outside, while the sky beyond was black. "Sorry… I'm sorry, I didn't mean to fall asleep while you were talking."

"Think nothing of it." She smiled.

"What time is it, anyway?"

"It must be after nine. I'm just know my dad is worried sick right that we're not back, yet." She gave a cross look at a bored looking, mustached man seated with his feet up on the sheriff's desk. The badge on the front of his blue police uniform told me this was the man we had been waiting all this time for. He didn't seem perturbed by her words. In fact, he didn't seem to care about anything much at all.

After that, Josie stiffly recounted the story of the attempted hold up earlier in the day, and I repeated the same story, though maybe in a friendlier tone. When Josie asked about the holdup man who had gotten away, the Sheriff only nodded and promised in a distracted voice that they'd get him.

Walking out into the warm night, crickets chirped out in the dark, while laughter and the sound of a happy melody playing on a piano could be heard from a nearby saloon. The mainstreet looked empty, and the windows of most storefronts were dark,

"He's not going to find the other guy." I shook my head as the door to the sheriff's office closed behind us.

"Probably not," Josie agreed. "Not unless the guy trips and falls into his lap."

I couldn't help but laugh.

"You were pretty brave today, punching that thug."

"Empty gun." I shrugged.

"You didn't know that." She gave my arm a squeeze.

"You were pretty brave hauling out that iron in the first place."

"My dad insists I have protection. Again, because he never had a boy, I was the one who he took out for target practice."

"Is that really the last thing you have of your mother's?" I motioned to the bag in her hand.

"Not at all," she said with a laugh. "I bought this cheap thing while passing through Montana, while I was on my way here to Washington."

"I suppose you don't want to keep your dad waiting," I said, trying to think if there was a lamp in the buckboard.

"I don't want to. But the livery stable must be closed, by now."

"Dammit, that's right!" I raised my face up to the starry night with a sigh, feeling hopelessly confounded.

"I think we should be able to find a hotel for tonight, after I call home."

***

The innkeeper, a sleepy eyed man who had been dozing behind the desk of his establishment, rented us a single room for the night, after we discovered we hadn't had enough for two. The second floor room as tiny, with a bed covered with off color sheets and pillow that smelled of sweat and dirt. I wouldn't have been surprised if bedbugs had colonized the mattress.

"Well, I'll take the floor," I offered, looking at the bare, hardwood planks.

"You'll do no such thing!" She stubornly laid the palms of her hands on her hips. "We both get into bed, or neither of us does."

"It wouldn't seem proper...," I stammered. "Your father..."

"Joe, my dad says you're one of the most honorable men he's ever known. Why else would he have you escort me?" Sitting down on the mattress, which creaked beneath her, she patted the dirty sheet and smiled. "So come on. We both need sleep."

Turning off the light switch, the room was cast in darkness, save for the lights of the town shining in from behind the curtains, when I climbed into bed next to Josie, both of us still fully clothed. The bed was tiny, obviously meant for a single person, and I could feel her warm body pressed against my back. I wondered if she could feel my heart pounding through my rib cage.

"Thank you for trusting me," I whispered.

"Joe… I like you a lot," she said softly from behind me. "And I think you like me."

"That I do."

"Joe, roll over to me."

I rolled over to face her in the dark, taking care not to fall off the bed. My eyes had adjusted to the dark enough to make out the grayish blur of her face.

"You are the most honorable man I know. On par with my dad, even." Putting her hands on the sides of my face, she moved closer to me. "But that doesn't mean I don't want this." Then her lips were on mine. I surrendered to her, both of us clumsily pulling off our clothes on the narrow mattress, before we were in each other's arms. My heart was beatiing wildly.

Who would have thought the events of the day, and having to spend the night together in Davenport, probably had saved Josie's life.

Chapter VI

The innkeeper's knock on the hotel room door at sun up, per
request following renting the room the night before, roused Josie and
me from our slumber. Sleepily, we both climbed slowly out of bed
with our stomach's rumbling, and our eyes blinking with the sunlight
streaming between the curtains, and got dressed. A diner was open
early to serve harvest bums, cowboys, and railroad men, where we
bought bacon, eggs, and hot coffee for breakfast, before we picked
up the buckboard wagon and rode out of town. For the longest time,
I remained quiet, my eyes fixed on the dirt road ahead of us, feeling
as if I had wronged her last night. She laid her hand on top mine that
held the reigns.

"What we did wasn't anything wrong, Joe," she said, as if able to
read my mind. "And if some folks think it was, well, they can go to
Hell!"

I laughed out loud at that last part, finally turning with the
courage to face her. "I'm a little scared of your dad. Not that I'm
going to trumpet what happened last night," I added quickly.

"Always the gentleman." She nodded with a smile.

"I'm just a little spooked about what he'll think about me after we
stayed in town all night."

"If anyone's in trouble for staying all night in town after going to mail a letter, it's me, and he didn't sound too happy when I called so late last night. I haven't been paddled by my dad since I was eight," Josie said, rubbing her bloodshot eyes as the wagon's wheels rolled over the uneven dirt road, causing the both of us to jostle about on the seat. "But I think I can expect one after missing bedtime last night." I almost would have taken her seriously from her tone of voice, were it not for her chuckle.

"I can't imagine Mr. Kahl laying an angry hand on you," I said cheerfully as I guided the horses' reigns. "Besides, it's too beautiful of a day to be thinking of whippin's." I motioned to the east as I spoke, where the dawn was rising beautifully but blindingly above the rolling sagebrush hills. The sunlight threw the shadows of the scrub pines sprouting here and there in this rough country.

A few hours later, we were back at the Kahl stead, when we both turned our heads to stare at the wagon we rode past, in which one of the horses was laid out in back, motionless and splattered with dried blood. The poor beast's head was barely attached by a flap of skin and red-black muscle to the ragged stump of it's neck, caked with congealed gore. With a gasp, Josie held her hand over her mouth.

"What happened?" she whispered, her shocked face turning pale. The fearless girl who had pulled a gun on would-be-robbers was suddenly shaken. I could only shake my head, stunned myself, as we rode on to the open barn door. The day didn't seem so wonderful, now.

We found McMurty inside, sweeping out the tell-tale bloodied straw from a stall where the door was wide open. His nose was still bent over from our fight weeks before. Leaping off the wagon, I asked, "What the hell happened here?"

Turning to me, he only shook his head, his normally ruddy complexion several shades paler, as well. "Must have been some sort of wild animal. Late last night, we heard a wild commotion coming from the barn, including the sound of the horse screaming."

Walking around the back of the wagon, I took Josie's hand and helped her to the ground as I listened to him.

"By the time we got here and lit our lanterns, the stall was open but the only trace of the animal was all this blood. We figured it had to be a horse theft gone wrong, till this morning when we found the horse out in the pastur with it's head almost ripped off, but no trace of whatever did it. You'd think only a bear could do that to something the size of a horse, but I've never heard of one this far out in the scablands."

Josie leaned close to me and almost whispered, "I'm going to find my dad, then get a change of clothes. Maybe a bath," before walking away quickly from the barn.

"Mr. Kahl's in the house," McMurty called after her. "He was pretty worried when she called she wouldn't be back last night," he told me in a lower tone when she was out of earshot.

"We got into a little scrape with a couple armed robbers," I explained, watching McMurty's eyes widen as I recounted the events from the day before. "By the time the damn sheriff got back to town to take our statements, it was already dark, so we stayed the night in town."

"You had enough for two rooms?"

"No, we only had enough for a single bed."

McMurty raised his eyebrows with a simple, "Hmm," and a slight smile.

"Oh, come on! You know it wasn't anything like that!" I lied.

"Just ribbin' you, kid," he slapped my shoulder. Had I known I'd gain McMurty's friendship by beating the shit out of him, I might have done it a lot sooner.

Mr. Kahl's tearfully happy voice, speaking German, made the two of us turn our heads, to see him embracing Josie in his arms just outside the front door of their house. She spoke soothingly to him in German, as well, returning his hug, before she went inside.

"And she was worried he'd be angry at her." I smiled.

"The old man's glad to have one less worry, I'd imagine," McMurty said. "With some animal or other killing one of the horses."

"Yoy tell him we found that stall door wide open, last night." It was Juliani who had been listening in, strolled over to us, turning his head to the dried blood spattered on the stall's wooden interior.

"Yeah." McMurty nodded. "What about it?"

Juliani shook his head. "I've never heard of any animal able to open a door."

"Dad! Dad!" It was Josie crying out, her hands pulling up on the hem of her dress as she ran from the house' door.

I rushed over to her, with McMurty and Juliani trailing behind me.

"Liebchen, what is it?" Mr. Kahl ran to her from the other direction, and caught her in his arms.

"My balcony doors…," she gasped for air, having run from the upstairs of the house. "They're wide open! I'm certain I had closed them before leaving for Davenport."

The sense of fear I felt begin to wash over me was stopped only by the icy numbness already there as the clear blue sky above seemed to lose it's brightness for me. I barely heard Mr. Kahl say we should go to the back of the house, and see if there was any evidence of a burglary, as memories of that night when I was twelve, threatened to flood back. *Of the glass paned, double doors wide open to the moonlight, and the harvest bum lying dead on the bed, with that thing…*

I tried to put that image out of my mind as I followed behind Mr. Kahl, Josie, Juliani, and McMurty to the other side of the house, reminding myself how, as a grown man, I knew what I had seen as a twelve ear old boy had only been fantasy.

"I think you'd need a ladder to get up there." McMurty looked up at the third floor balcony. Turning his head back, he asked, "Were there any marks on the balcony's edge a ladder might leave, Miss Josie?"

"No." She shook her head. "Not that I noticed."

"Are you okay, Joseph?" Mr. Kahl looked at me with concern. "You look white as a sheet."

I nodded quickly. "I'm fine," I said, more abruptly than I had intended.

Josie smiled and gently touched my hand. She knew what was running through my mind. "I probably just left it open, and forgot."

"Make sure nothing's missing," Mr. Kahl said to her, giving the open balcony doors one last look.

"It's okay, Joe," she whispered to me as the others walked away. "I'm sure I just forgot."

I nodded wordlessly. As we walked away, I glanced back at that odd, misshapen, brick building with it's sealed door, in the distance, cast it's shadow in the sun over head.

Chapter VII

For the next few weeks, as the daylight lasted longer and it got warmer with summer, there weren't anymore attacks on the animals, or evidence of further break ins. The boys smiled and nodded when they'd catch Josie and me with our head close together as we'd laugh and talk in low voices, or when we'd walk away, hand-in-hand. I didn't think Mr. Kahl noticed, as he never said a thing. I couldn't imagine he'd be pleased with his daughter consorting with a penniless harvest bum like me. But he never even batted an eye when Josie invited me to come along with them to the local Lutheran church on Sunday. Seeing how I looked lost, sitting there in the pew as all the hymms and sermon were in German, Josie whispered to me she'd help me learn the language. That was fine for me, as the only German I had learned so far were cuss words from Mr. Kahl. For the first time in a very long time, I was sincerely happy.

There was more than enough work to do around the Kahl place to keep the rest of us occupied, tending the cattle and other animals to keep us all busy. With the harvest coming up, Mr. Kahl would pay us our lump wages after selling wheat and cattle at market, and that made us hired hands appreciative. The harvest at the end of the season, when the weather would grow cooler, was always in the back of our minds, as that meant most of us could expect to be laid off. But for now, with plenty of good food and a place to sleep, and enough sunshine overhead, that might as well have been a million years away. Then I learned of a whole other reason to wish that Fall would never come.

I was in the barn, shoveling horseshit and straw from one of the horse stalls, when Josie walked inside. "Need some help?" she offered, her face bright with a smile. She had traded her skirt and blouse for faded overalls and a plaid shirt. Her brown hair was braided into pigtails.

I stopped work to lean on the shovel's handle, it's metal scoop coated with manure laced straw, pressed against the ground, and my eyes took her in. There was something that went beyond a look of relaxation about her now that she was dressed in men's work clothes. As if the skirts and blouses she had worn before had required her to play the role of sophisticate that she would rather be free of.

"You like my look?" She spun around with a grin in front of me, as if she knew what I had been thinking. "It took forever for my dad to let me dress like I had as a kid. He thinks I ought to look like a lady all the time."

"Uh.. Yeah… sure, you can lend me a hand," I said, feeling awkwardly foolish, again. I grinned clumsily while adjusting my hat.

Grabbing a pitchfork from the corner, she worked the stalls on the other side of the barn. "Joe? Remember how I mentioned how my dad's been talking about getting me into college in Chicago?"

I nodded. "Sure I do." She had talked about furthering her education those evenings we had sat on her balcony, watching the sun sink in the horizon. It was a thing almost unheard of for a woman to study at university level, but it was a dream she had spoken of more than once.

"There's… uh… something else I figured I should tell you." She breathed a sigh. "My dad just surprised me with news he's been able to gain me admission to college. Out pastor has influential friends, it seems." Her eyes fell to the barn floor. "Again, I'm getting the attention he'd shower on a son. I'll... be leaving for school in Chicago this September." Her chuckle was sad and humorless.

I nodded, putting on my best poker face to hide my disappointment. "A woman going to college is something pretty noteworthy." I tried to smile. "You shouldn't let a chance like that get away." I suppose I had let my feelings for her give way to impossible daydreams of the two of us tying the knot, and settling down to raise a herd of children. Penniless harvest bums like me didn't get to marry the boss' daughter in real life.

"Joe, I don't know if I want to go to school," her voice became small as she frowned. "I mean… growing up, all I could think about was getting away from farming out in the middle of nowhere. But now… somewhere along the line, I've come to love this life and the land I have it in." She turned her face to the barn's open doorway, and seemed to be seeing beyond just the Kahl farm, to the rough land of sagebrush and broken rock, settled with rough men and women she had become part of. She turned back to me. "Most of all, I don't want to go because I found you here."

I imagined her arms were around my neck, pulling my lips to hers, swearing her love and devotion to me. Maybe a poor farmhand could get the girl, after all, my imaginary self thought, squeezing her tightly.

Drooping her head, she sadly closed her eyes. "But this might be a once in a life time opportunity that I just can't pass up."

I nodded wordlessly, hoping tears wouldn't crack through my poker face.

***

I was fast asleep in the bunkhouse with the rest of the boys, when a woman's screams caused me to waken and bolt upright in the dark.

"Josie!" was the first word out of my mouth, as I threw the sheet off myself and leaped out of the top bunk.

"What was that?" McMurty sleepily sat up in the bunk below me.

"I think that was Josie screaming!"

By the tme the other boys were stirring out of bed, I was already out the door and racing in my long johns toward the house. There, I pounded my fist against the front door, calling out: "Josie! Mr. Kahl! What's wrong?" The other hands gathered behind me, wearing just their long underwear. It took several minutes till Mr. Kahl opened the door, the lamp in his hand spilling a yellowish light on all of us.

"Mr. Kahl, what happened?" I heard the desperation in my own voice.

"It's alright… It's alright." He raised a calming hand to me. "Josie just had a very bad nightmare."

"It wasn't a nightmare," Josie's voice, low and shaken, came from behind her father. "I know the difference between a dream and real life." She walked into view of the open door, wearing only a white nightgown.

Looking over his shoulder, he spoke gently to her in German, and she answered back in the same, her face falling into her hands as she broke into tears.

"Thank you for your concern," Mr. Kahl said softly as he closed the door. "It'll be alright."

"Something was trying to open the balcony doors to my room!"
she cried out in English. "I saw it! It was horrible!"

I felt fright tingle down my spine, as memories of that thing, on
top of that the dead bindle stiff, feeding on him in the darkness… in
her very bedroom, flashed through my head.

She wiped her eyes. "Dad… can Joe stay with me, tonight?"

"What? Stay here… with you?" Mr. Kahl looked from Josie to
me, then back to Josie, the befuddled look on his face bordering on
anger.

McMurty coughed behind me to stifle a laugh, which brought me
back to the present. I kicked backward, feeling my heel land hard
against his shin. He grunted with pain and amusement.

The unhuman cry turned all our heads to the darkness.

"It's coming from the pasture!" Gary shouted. We all ran out into
the darkness, with Mr. Kahl leading the way with his lamp, when his
feet skidded to a stop at the fence penning in the cattle.

"Mein Gott!" Mr. Kahl exclaimed, as the rest of us stopped short
of running into him. I saw his face turn pale in the yellow lamp light
at the sight of the the bellowing cow's front half that ended in
bloody entrails spilled across the grass. The back half laid lifelessly
behind, feces emptied over her rear legs and the ground. Attempting
to push herself up on her remaining front legs, the cow's scream was
almost human, when she collapsed. The lamp light reflected off the
lifeless, open eyes.

Juliani was the first to turn away. The rest of us could hear him
vomiting in the darkness as we could only stare, as if our brains
couldn't register the extent of this horror.

"Holy shit!" McMurty was the first to speak, his voice shrill as
he ran his splay fingered hands down his face. "What could've done
this? A bear? A wolf?"

"Aint no animal that did this," Cranston's voice was almost a
whisper from behind us. We turned our heads to listen to him.
"Whatever did this wasn't killing for food." His trembling finger
pointed at the ripped in half animal laying in the circle of yellowish
light. "What did this was angry, and just wanted to kill."

"You four men, McMurty, Cranston, Juliani, and Gary," Mr. Kahl
said, turning to us, and held his lamp high. I had never seen this man
shake with fright before, which was just as horrifying as any thing

else I had seen that night. "I'd like you to get your guns and keep watch with me for the rest of the night."

And me? All that time, I stood in silence at the edge of the light, as thoughts of, *What I saw way back when wasn't real... It couldn't be real... It can't be real... But it somehow is...* swirled through my brain.

"Joe?" Mr. Kahl looked to me with growing anxiety.

"Huh?" I shook my head to clear those thoughts away. Yes, sir?"

"I'd like you to get your gun, too, and go inside and keep Josie safe."

***

Walking back in the dark from the bunk house with my rifle, I saw light glowing from the bottom floor of the main house' windows. *It somehow knew Josie was in the top floor bedroom,* I thought as I approached the front door. *When it first came for her, she had been away with me in Davenport. Driven by some instinct to kill and feed, it attacked one of the horses, instead,* realization dawned on me. *Tonight, it found her in bed, but she had scared it off.* Remembering what Cranston had said, I knew it must have been filled with unbelievable rage for not having been able to take Josie when it ripped that cow in half.

Opening the door, the first thing I saw was the revolver in Josie's hand pointed at me. She stared at me from the living room couch, her jaw dropped open and her eyes filled with terror, seemingly unable to recognize me.

I raised my hands. "It's me! It's just me!"

A moment later, she dropped the gun to the cushioned seat, and half laughed, half cried. "Joe, I could have shot you." She ran a free hand down her face with relief.

"Sorry, I should've known better to knock, first," I appologized as I sat down next to her. She scooted over to me, pressed her head against my chest, and put her arms around me. I had imagined I don't know how many times that she would seek safety in my arms as one who could give her love and protection. But, God, not in a nightmare like this.

I put my arm around her, and felt how she trembled. "It's alright. You're safe," I told her softly. "Your dad's outside with the boys, keeping an eye on the cattle. They'll kill it in case what ever it was comes back."

"I saw it, Joe," she choked, tearfully. "It was horrible! I woke up when I heard hinges squeak, and saw it in the moonlight coming through the doors to the balcony."

"What... was it?" My voice became hoarse, despite myself, as fright rose inside me.

"It was almost just a shadow in what light came from outside, but what I saw… it looked almost like a skeleton. But it had flesh over it's bones, like those Union army prisoners from Andersonville, back in Civil War days." She looked up from my chest, and I saw how her eyes, set in a face drained of color and wet with tears, were wide with fright. "Joe… The thing you saw as a boy, in this house… I think I saw the same thing."

She buried her face into my long john shirt, again, and I held her tightly. And there, I sat awake all night holding her, even after she had eventually fallen asleep. My other hand remained on my rifle, the business end of it's barrel resting against the floor. My own heart thumping beneath my ribcage was the only sound in the house' otherwise dead silence, as my eyes roved from the front door, to the windows, and to the staircase. Especially the staircase, as I waited expectantly for that Godless thing I had seen as a half grown kid come down the steps. For most of my life, from that night in 1902, till the sunset this summer, I lived with crippling fear that left me broken and always ready to run away. But now, even as terrified as I was, the reason I had to stand my ground and fight that nameless creature was slumbering in the crook of my arm. Even though in another month, I knew she'd probably be leaving for a whole new life without me in it.

I only let myself fall asleep when the dawn's first rays shined through the windows.

Chapter IIX

That day, I put a lock on the inside of the balcony's double, glass paned doors for Josie.

"Thank you," she breathed with relief, watching me work. I heard the bed springs squeak as she stood up from the edge of the bed behind me. "Now, let's see if I have the courage to ever sleep in here again," she chuckled humorlessly as she walked over to join me.

Her room was a library in itself, with the walls lined with book shelves containing everything from literature, to science, to history, at least by the English language titles I saw. I assumed the books in German were the same.

"It's probably a good idea you sleep with your gun nearby," I said, glancing over my shoulder from where I was crouching as she came up behind me. Finishing up re-tightening the screws for a second time, I stood up. "Has your dad said anything to you about last night?"

She shook her head. "He knows something killed one of the cows last night, but he's still insistent I was only having a nightmare about something trying to get in." Barking a laugh, she said, "He doesn't want to believe in anything he can't see or touch, so much so, I think he hardly even believes in God."

"Believing that would make things a lot simpler, I suppose." I cracked a lop sided smile.

"From what I've been hearing outside this morning, the hired men don't want to stick around after last night." All pretense of good humor left her face for worry. "I don't know what my dad's going to do with them bailing on him."

"I'm sticking around," I assured her. I only wished she would stay here with me, too, but I let that go unsaid.

A scratching, rustling sound came from the ceiling. Both Josie and I looked up. "Rats or some other varmints up there," I said. "Remind me to go up there to roust it out," remembering the strange little door between the balcony and the roof, and the attic space it must open up to.

Immediately, the sound stopped.

Josie chortled, "Guess it must have heard you."

***

"I need you boys," I heard Mr. Kahl say to Cranston and Juliani as I walked across the yard to the bunkhouse, where the three of them stood outside of. McMurty stood away from them at the other end of the bunk house, his head down and looking troubled, while Gary leaned out of the building's open doorway, his round, dark face hard and unreadable. "I can't get the harvest in without a full crew." It was as close to begging as I had ever heard from the boss. "Besides," he explained, with hands extended with open palms. "I don't have any money to pay you till I make a sale at market this Fall."

"I couldn't give a shit about my pay." Cranston's voice trembled with fear and growing anger as he shook his head emphatically. "Money isn't gonna do me any good if I'm not alive to spend it. You should be leaving here, too, especially after that thing tried to get into your daughter's room last night."

"And I told you already, Josie had a bad dream that had nothing to do with what happened to that cow," Mr. Kahl said wearily, as if he had been repeating that again and again to deaf ears. Turning to Juliani, he asked, "Are you set on leaving, too?"

"Sorry, boss," Juliani muttered, keeping his eyes down on the ground as with shame. Both hobos had their meager belongings wrapped up in their bindles tied to the ends of their walking sticks.

Mr. Kahl nodded dolefully. "I can't make you boys stay." Stirring the dirt under foot with the the toe of his work boot, he said softly, "Well, if either of you change your minds, you both have jobs here."

Mumbling his thanks with averted eyes, Juliani turned to join Cranston, who was already walking away.

Sidling up to Mr. Kahl, I growled sternly, "Goddamn ingrates," watching their backs as they headed toward the road. Gary stepped out from the Bunkhouse, and joined us.

"They're just scared." Mr. Kahl pursed his lips with a look of understanding. "I suppose I probably would be, too, if I didn't have a stake in this place."

Turning my head, I said, "McMurty?" The cowpuncher had been standing away from the rest of us, silently, almost forgotten. "You staying?"

"I'm sorry, I can't." I heard the fear in McMurty's voice, and saw how his ruddy complexion had paled. "Like Cranston said, no amount of money's worth getting killed for. Not when that thing can rip an animal that size in half."

"I figured you'd be yellow," Gary said dismissively, as he looked away with contempt.

"Who you callin' yellow, redskin?" McMurty's face darkened again, his eyes flaring with anger. Snatching the hat from the top of his head, he threw it to the ground.

"You, you tub of yellow shit!" Stabbing a finger in the air as he walked toward the cowboy, Gary snapped, "Next time you even think about shitting on my people again, you just remember it was an Indian who stayed when you ran away with your tail between your legs!"

McMurty rushed at Gary with a roar, when Mr. Kahl quickly stepped in between them. "Enough!" he shouted, with both hands raised in a peace making gesture. "I'm not having…" he started to say, when the angry man collided into him, knocking him down.

"Boss!" Gary's feet stopped in mid step to turn around to Mr. Kahl, who sat on the ground, the wind knocked out of him, when McMurty grabbed him by the shirt collar with both hands, and threw him face forward to the dusty ground. Gary's wide brimmed hat tumbled off his head.

"I'll show you who's yellow!" He booted Gary in the ribs just as he rolled to his side, causing him to curl up in pain with a groan.

That's when I lunged at the big cowboy, my arms around his barrel thick waist as I spun him around and slammed him to the ground with a thud. I saw the startled look on his face as he stared up at me.

"Stay down, Goddamn it!" I told him, raising a clenched fist when he tried to sit back up. "Stay down. I don't want to hurt you, again, but I will." Raising his hands in surrender, he nodded and let his head fall back, panting for air. I walked over to Mr. Kahl, and offered him a hand to pull himself back up. "Are you alright, boss?"

"Ja... I think so." He nodded, brushing dust from his overalls.

"He called me yellow," McMurty's low voice trembled. Having stood up, he turned his face away from us, his chest heaving with each heavy breath he took. I realized he was close to bursting into tears.

"McMurty?" I took a step forward, only for him to turn his back to me. Quickly, he wiped his eyes.

"I'm scared, too, McMurty." Gary's voice had become unexpectedly gentle. Wincing, he let Mr. Kahl help him up while holding the side of his ribcage with the other hand. "I don't know what pulled that cow in half last night, and I'm sure it could do the same to any of us. But I'm not going to run away. I'm for killing it before any of us die."

McMurty nodded, turning back around, but still unable to face any of us. "I guess I'll stay," his voice was hoarse, and a lump rose in his throat. "At least for now."

"Thank you," Mr. Kahl whispered to Gary, with a nod and a smile.

"Dad? I just got a call from the Davenport post office."

We all turned to Josie, who was walking from the main house, unnoticed for all the drama playing out between us men.

"A letter came from Seattle. I think Mr. Nagy's relative there wrote back to us."

***

The ride with Josie to Davenport, and back to the Kahl spread again, was much less eventful than the previous trip. She had put on a long, summery dress, and a plumed, wide brimmed hat meant for keeping the sun out of her eyes. For the most part, I sat quietly with reigns in hand, eyes fixed forward on the road ahead of us, till Josie finally said, "You're not talking to me, again."

"I don't know what to say." I answered softly with a shrug, and that was the God's honest truth. I wanted to tell her how I had hoped she was the one meant for me, only to have her dash that notion along with my heart. But men don't know how to be tender and bare their hearts. Goddamn it.

Closing her eyes she lowered her head before speaking, again. "I never wanted to cause you any hurt, Joe." Turning her face to the miles of empty scabland beyond the road that stretched to the horrizon, her voice was almost a whisper: "I wasn't thinking when we…," she began to say, before she shook her head, as if searching for the right words. "I hadn't intended to toy with your heart. And I was wrong to, because I already knew I was going to be leaving for school if I could."

I blinked tears from my eyes as we rode along, unable to say another word to keep my heart ache inside. Josie sat beside me, quiet as well, with a sad frown on her face.

Chapter IX

That evening, Mr. Kahl rapped his fist lightly on the bunkhouse door before coming inside. Setting aside the magazine I was reading, I swung my legs off the edge of my bunk and sat up. Yellow light from the gas lantern hanging by the door threw his shadow down the aisle between the bunk beds, and made the lines of age on his somber face stand out. "Boys?"

Gary set the rifle he was cleaning on the mattress he was sitting on, while McMurty looked up from whittling in the bunk below mine.

Mr. Kahl put his hands behind his back, and lowered his eyes. "Josie asked me to come get you," he said softly. "Because you three chose to stay with us, she thought it was only right for you to be included for a reading of the letter sent to us."

***

The three of us joined the Kahls in their living room, having taken our seats in front of the darkened fireplace where Josie stood, wearing the dress she had on when I had taken her to Davenport earlier. In her hand was the envelope she and I had picked up at the Davenport post office earlier in the day, the edge of which she anxiously tapped against her empty palm. Mr. Kahl joined me on the sofa with a subdued expression. The electric lights on the ceiling above made the world outside the windows pitch black. When Josie's eyes moved across the faces before her, then stopped to linger on mine with a smile on her lips, I felt my heart pulse bittersweetly.

Clearing her throat, she began: "This is a letter from Katarina Phelps of Seattle, who is a cousin of Victor Nagy, the man who had built this house, and had formerly owned the property. She assured me she and her husband, who she married after immigrating from Hungary, have no interest in the property, particualarly since, by the rules of the Homestead Act, they have no legal claim. But there's another reason why she wants nothing to do with the house and land. The things she wrote to me of… I could hardly believe such a thing, till I took into consideration the things that have been happening on this farm. The least of which happened last night, when something tried to break into my room, then killed another of our animals."

I glanced at Mr. Kahl, and saw the regret on his face as he slumped his head.

"I will dispense with the legal matters in question," she continued, as she removed the pages from the envelope, and unfolded them, "and I'll get right to the story Katarina conveyed to me."

Chapter X

Katarina Phelps' Tale.

Much of what I am about to convey has come to me second hand, but I have no reason to doubt any of it. My cousin, Victor Ferdinand Nagy, was born in 1865, to a family - my family - that boasted of it's heritage of minor Hungarian nobility. He and his older brother, Bela, had grown up in a rural, backwater province that was worlds away from sophisticated, cosmopolitan Budapest, where my parents had raised me. Of the few times I met Victor and his brother in my lifetime, the first had been when we had been children. My mother had just passed away, and my father, needing an escape from his grief, told me I would visit our cousins in the country while he traveled to Vienna. When he had told me my relations resided in a castle, that alone excited my imagination with images of princesses in colorful dresses, and bold knights in armor charging on horseback.

So, at age ten, my father took me from Hungary's capital, with it's libraries, symphonies, art galeries, and overall high culture I had been raised in, for a land of small villages tucked away amid dark forests and lonely plains. There, I discovered a world I hardly knew existed. People, usually illiterate, often ridden with sickness, and chained by superstition as much by their low status poverty, worked themselves to the bone from sun up to sun down, just to barely survive. To my shame, I had learned much of what their endless toil was exploited by businesses run by not just the bourgeois business owners, but also on the farmland the local nobles where they resided as tenants and dependants. Nobles that included my relatives. Since, I have always been grateful that my grandfather had chosen to raise his sons in Budapest, far away from that shadowed, backward place, where cruel, powerful men felt justified by the rank they had been born into, or by the riches they had attained, to take from people who had almost nothing.

The ancient castle, where Victor and his brother grew up, was perched along a rocky summit, above a cluster of little villages, where the people living there worked in the nearby fields. The reality of the small, drafty fortress erected centuries ago, bore no resemblance to what I had fantasized. Even less so did my kin living within it's crumbling walls. My uncle Josef, with his steely eyes and gray streaked beard, was a hard man with little tolerance for the peasants who he overworked. He saw them as almost a different bloodline, a different race even, from his own Maygar lineage. He also had no compunction when it came to physically disciplining his two sons. More than once, he had even felt free to beat me with a leather strap he kept on hand for doling out punishment.

It had been my happy, carefree cousin, Bela, who became my best friend when I was there, even though I was closer to Victor's age. Bela would escape into another world beyond his demanding father through what books were in the castle. A world he allowed me into when we read stories or histories aloud to one another during those days. That time of my life when I had lost my mother, and had been all but deserted by my father, he made bearable, even happy. Marriages between cousins was no disgrace in those days, and I suppose I had hoped I could someday bring Bela, with his head of curls and gentle face, back to Budapest with me as my husband. But no such childhood dreams of mine ever saw the light of day.

But Victor, was a whole other story. Having learned from his father too well, he had become the terror of the local village children, bullying and intimidating them for what little money or toys they had. He was the lord's son, after all, and few dared to complain. It had only been Bela who had taken their part. More often than not, he had been left bleeding and at the mercy of Victor's fists for his trouble, despite being the older brother. But on some occassions, Victor would join Bela and me with the local children in one of the darkened village hovels, when a village elder would regail us all with the folk tales and legends in that part of Hungary. I still recall the fire throwing flickering shadows across a wizened face, and eyes expresively widening or narrowing as the tale was told in a voice creaking with age. Very often, their stories could freeze the blood of us young listeners, telling us of ghosts, and werewolves, and of the vampires that drank the blood of the living. Perhaps most frightening of those old people's stories was that such monsters had once been men or women who had had lost their humanity to become the thing at night, outside the window. But I had been brought up in the modern city of Budapest, and even at that age, I believed those stories that gave me the shivers were nothing more than the superstitions of my ancestors that were best left in the past.

***

After more than half a year, my father had sent a message for me to return to him in Budapest, complete with a carriage ride to the nearest train station. Bela had been the only thing I had regret for leaving behind in that backward, forgotten place.

It wouldn't be till almost ten years later till I saw either of the Nagy brothers, again. This time, it was for their father's funeral, that I accompanied my own father back to the Nagy's ancestral castle. Besides the few relatives assembled there, the local people had been told attendance at the funeral was mandatory by my cousin, Victor. I saw little in the way of real grief among them for my uncle's death. The terrifying man who had beaten me as a child almost as often he did his sons, was now almost unrecognizable laid out in the open coffin. Looking like a skeleton with skin stretched over his bones, my Uncle Josef's beard, and hair that now sparsely covered his head, had greyed, and his hands folded on his chest looked like boney claws. I was more than relieved when his coffin was shut, and interred in the family crypt.

Little had changed from when I was a child visiting there, though such hidden away places tend to be fixed in time. But one thing that had changed was Bela, now himself a stranger returning home. Though the eldest son who had been meant to inherit his father's lands, he had chosen to leave home and study art and literature in Vienna, now the capitol of our country since Hungary had become one with Austria. Leaving his predigree and title in the past, he had chosen to live a bohemian life among writers, musicians, and artists in the Austrian-Hungarian Empire's leading city. He had told me his brother was welcome to the cold, decaying castle, as that was part of a world he wanted nothing more to do with. Also, he had confided in me that, with the nature of his love life he found among his happy, free spirited peers, it was unlikely he'd ever produce an heir of his own. He had no illusions that he could ever be accepted for his "love none dare speak," if he ever returned home to stay. I have to admit, what remained of the girl I had been who had dreams of romance with Bela, felt disappointment deep down, knowing he would never be mine.

But of course, this is Victor's story. My eldest cousin had remained silent and aloof for the funeral, and for the short time I had stayed there. Though dark and handsome in his manhood, his hard eyes, and the grim frown he wore, were much like the memories I had of his and Bela's father. Bela had told me Victor was of two minds about his inheritance. Their father had beaten notions of duty and responsibility into him when it came to the upkeep of his ancestral lands. And yet, that same sense of obligation had hung around his neck like a millstone that filled him with resentment. Resentment for the peasants who hated him, and who were leaving when they could for Budapest, or Vienna, or America. And resentment for the downward slide of the family's wealth toward eventual poverty, as the land he had been tasked with produced less and less with the loss of manpower, as his hereditary title came to mean less and less in the modern world. I have often wondered if he envied his free spirited brother who had escaped that place that belonged in the past.

But there had been something else Bela said Victor had confided in him about, one night when they had shared five or six bottles of wine to toast the passing of their monster father. Victor had been with Josef the whole time he was dying of bowel cancer. It was a malady some think was as much an inheritance of the Nagy family as was the castle and their land, as others of our line had been claimed by it as far back as collective memory reached. His subdued voice slurring with too much alcohol, Victor had recounted how it had first started with how their father complained about stomach pains that only grew worse, doubling him over when the agony came. Soon after, he hadn't been able to keep down food, and there was blood after he used the chamber pot.

Victor had brought in a doctor, who his father only grudgingly allowed to perform an examination. The results the doctor gave only had confirmed what Josef already guessed was happening to him. More and more duties were taken up by Victor, as their father had become increasingly frail. In the end, he had become a living skeleton, vomiting blood over the front of his nightshirt. Too weak to make use of the chamber pot without help, his bed was often befouled with bloody feces and urine. Victor had always believed he hated his father, but he found himself breaking down in tears as he prayed – not for God to heal his father any longer – but to end his pain. That had been when Victor brought a pistol to his father's bed chamber, and offered him a way out of suffering.

"No, it's a mortal sin," his father had wheezed as blood oozed from his lips down his chin, pushing away the gun Victor tried to hand him. Setting the gun aside, Victor admitted to Bela he had taken the pillow from under their father's head, and pushed it down over his face. Josef had feebly thrashed his legs about, and tried to pull away Victor's hands pressing down on the pillow. It had taken longer than Victor had expected, but in the end, their father's limbs fell back on the bed and were still. When he had removed the pillow, he had found the other side stained with blood, saliva, and vomit, while their father's eyes stared emptily at the ceiling.

His dark complexion having paled, Victor's frightened eyes stared ahead as if at a future only he could see. "I will never let myself die like that," he had whispered to Bela, as well as to himself. "Not robbed of dignity, covered with bloody sick and shit." That rest of the night, Bela had conducted a one sided conversation after his brother had fallen into silence, downing more and more wine till he eventually passed out.

Shaking his head sadly, Bela had told me he didn't believe his father's ailment could ever have been cured, but had he gone to Budapest or Vienna, he at least could have been under constant medical care, and might have died with a degree of peace. Instead, Josef had remained in a place centuries out of step with the rest of the modern world, and died wretchedly as people in such places eventually do.

After three days, I was ready to leave that sad, hidden away place, when Bela escorted me to the village where I would wait for a carriage to take me to the nearest railroad depot. What met us there were raised voices coming from one of the small houses. One we both clearly recognized as Victor's, alternating between pleading and rage, while the other was the rusty voice of an old woman, shouting back with anger. When I asked Bela what was happening, he only shook his head, and suggested somebody might have been late with rent.

The door to the hovel was thrown open, and out stomped maybe the oldest crone I had ever seen, her shriveled face shrouded by the black kerchief tied around her gray hair. Following at her heels was Victor, his hands outstretched as he begged her: "I'll give you anything! You can live her free of rent for the rest of your life. Just tell me!"

The frail old woman had fearlessly whirled about with frenzied eyes, as if Victor was her equal and not her hereditary landlord, and screamed into his face: "I told you, I'll not damn myself by damning you!" She had stormed away, leaving Victor, with shoulders slumped, to stare despairingly at the ground, seemingly oblivious to the other villagers who had come out their doors to stare.

Watching after the old woman walking away, Bela whispered to me that he couldn't believe she was still alive, after all these years. Shaking my head, I had asked him who she was. He had answered: "That's Magda. She's the last of the village old people who used to frighten us three as children with stories about things that go bump in the night."

Getting on board the carriage that soon after arrived, I never learned that day what Victor had wanted from Magda. But years later, that would change.

***

Five years later, I had been swept off my feet by a dashing American engineer named David Phelps, whose reputation preceded him for his much sought after work for bridges and railroads he had built in Berlin, Paris, Vienna, and finally, my own Budapest. We had met in the same elite social circles, and I found myself drawn to his frank, Yankee directness, and his uninhibited, boisterous laughter that was so unlike the sophisticated but inhibited world I knew. Though regarded to be uncouth by the European gentry, I was smitten, even though he was almost twenty years my senior. I soon found he had also been infatuated by me, which led to his asking for my hand in marriage.

With David's assignment coming to a close in Budapest, we made plans for me to accompany him to Seattle, where he planned on establishing a firm of his own, folllowing our nuptials. At our wedding, I met Bela again, now having put on some weight, who I had been sent an invitation to. With him was his "friend," a tall, blond German artist named Fritz Hanke, who he now lived with in Beriln. Looking about the guests filling the dining hall where the reception was held, I had asked where Victor was, as I had also been invited him. His face paling, Bela said: "Ask me tomorrow. Now is not the time for such an unhappy story."

The next day, I called him at his hotel, and made arrangements to meet for lunch despite that this was the time for my honeymoon. We met at the patio of a downtown Budapest cafe, where we had exchanged pleasantries, laughing as we caught up since we had last seen each other as we ate. That was when I had asked about Victor.

Bela's cheerful mood turned grave. He told me the invitation doubtlessly had ended up in limbo, as he had found Victor had since deserted the castle, leaving a caretaker named Gregor to manage the sale of the farm produce, and the rest of the financials. Shaking his head sadly, Bela said, "All for a reason I at first thought could only be described as mad. Now I know it could only be called evil." I

remember how his food had grown cold and unfinished as he told his
story…

***

On occasion, a rare letter from his younger brother would reach
Bela, making him hope Victor had freed himself from their dead
father's shakles of hereditary duty and responsibility, and was
leading the happy life of a world traveler. But then, he had seen how
the letters were postmarked from the hidden away corners of Europe,
as well as Victor's descriptions of places filled with abject poverty
and ignorance, differing little from where the two brothers had
grown up. Much of what he wrote had been centered around fears
that cancer was growing inside his bowels, as it had with their father
and other Nagys, which would ravage him before ending his life. He
obsessed that time had been running out for him before he could find
his salvation among the secretive, old peasants who understood the
stories of the long past hadn't been just stories. When Bela asked
him exactly what sort of salvation he had been looking for, the
letters stopped, perhaps with Victor realizing that he had said too
much. After that, his heart had been constantly filled with worry for
Victor, growing fearful his brother's fixation with his own eventual
death was carrying him to a dark place in his own mind. When
meeting travelers, he would inquire if they had seen or heard of
Victor Nagy, with no success.

It had only been an accident that Bela was able to locate his
brother a few years later. He had just met Fritz, and the two had
been attending a party in a loft turned into a studio, thrown by
another artist, following his successful art show in Prague. It had
been there that a drunken French poet by the name of Emile Perot, a
short, rotund fellow with a pencil thin mustache, was talking
boisterously to anyone who would listen. When his audience grew
bored with him and turned away, he soon talked at the top of his
voice to keep their attention, as he went on about the time his train
had stalled in the mountainous borderland between Walachia and
Transylvania. It had been then that Bela heard him describe how he
had chosen to stretch his legs and look for something to drink in the
nearby village. There, he had run into a mad Hungarian with wild

hair and beard, and whose finely tailored suit of clothes he wore
hung loosely on his rail thin body. This man had haunted the homes
of the local old people, making a nuisance of himself as he paid them
fists full of cash to recount their secrets of the nosferatus. Laughing,
he had shaken his head at the memory.

"What? Who was this mad Hungarian?" Bela had asked, raising
his own voice above the chatter as he abruptly turned away from
their host with whom Fritz and he had been conversing with, to press
through the other guests to reach the Perot. Seemingly more
interested in hearing his own voice, the French poet ignored the
question and turned away and went on about some other subject,
when Bela had grabbed him by his lapels and pulled him only inches
away from his face, leaving the surrounding artists and writers
aghast. Aghast at himself, in fact, as he had never known himself to
have displayed such rage before. "The Hungarian, what was his
name?" Bela had demanded, shaking him like a rag doll. "Was his
name Victor Nagy?"

Mouth agape dumbly with fright, Perot had finally stammered
that yes, that was the man's name. From there, he had tearfully
answered every question Bela had put to him: such as that had been
almost four weeks ago when he had last seen Victor, giving Bela the
name of the village. After he had finally released his hold on Perot's
dinner jacket, the Frenchman scurried out the door, at the applause
of the host and his guests, happy to be rid of the noisy Gallic bore.

Days later, after promising Fritz he'd be back to him, soon, Bela
was on a passenger train headed to Walachia and Transylvania.
Gone was the modernity of the cities of the European west where he
had chosen to make his home, giving way to the backward, forest
shrouded countryside so much like that of the childhood he had
escaped. There at the village the pompous Frenchman had given
him the name of, he learned from the locals of the mad Hungarian
named Nagy, who had been constantly writing in a ledger as he
pressed the oldest people for what they knew of unspeakable,
forbiden things. Things about the dead who hadn't stayed in the
grave, but rose to prey on the living. But that had been weeks
before, Nagy having since left for even more remote hamlets where
he hoped to learn more of the damned.

Following after, Bela traveled through the narrow mountain roads twisting through dark forests, sometimes by carriage, other times by wagon, or just on horse back. He would learn he had just missed his brother by a week in one village, and then by mere days in the next, and the next after that. Always, the things Victor sought to know from the ancients who kept the stories alive, chilled the local people to the bone, making them grateful he had gone on his way. And then he came to the town where, much to his excitement, he had been told by a village headman how Victor had visited twice in a matter of days. The first time, Victor had been told that the people in a village miles away had captured one of the creatures he had been searching for – surely a crazy story given too much credence, Bella had thought. He left, and then was back a few days later, offering money to the villagers to send someone with him. They gave him the town whore in exchange for a wad of money. That had been the last time any of them had lain eyes on the haggard foreigner with the haunted look, or the woman they had sent with him.

Following the directions given to him from the last village, Bela had thought he had become lost on roads that turned into hardly more than foot paths through the woods, till he came upon the cluster of hovels within a valley surrounded by mountain crags. The few people living there had looked sickly and underfed, their worn, dirty garments hanging loosely on their scarecrow thin bodies. When he had asked about his brother, one of the villagers, a dwarfish grey beard named Vlad, who his neighbors called the key holder, nodded sadly, recalling the mad man who first came to see the nosferatu they had captured.

He told Victor of how the thing had preyed on their children, night after night, causing the young ones to waste away till death. And then one night, the creature had been caught the monster in the act, draining the life from the last living child as she slept. The villagers could have killed it, but something worse was more deserving. Holding it down and hacking off it's limbs, they had locked it away to suffer without blood to nourish it, as it cried out in anguish day and night. Victor insisted on seeing the creature, as if it was part of a carnival show. After spending hours in the shack where it was kept, Victor had left, only to return days later, this time with a simple mongoloid girl in tow.

When Victor had demanded they unlock the chains on the door, and his intention with the poor, backward girl with the snub nose and dull, slanted eyes had become clear, Vlad the key holder told him to leave, wanting no part in the godless thing he was about to do. That only earned Vlad a beating at Victor's hands, followed by the pistol the Hungarian madman had pulled out of his coat pocket, and placed at his head. In the end, Victor had gotten the key to open the lock. Shoving the girl in first, he closed the door behind them. The man wept unashamedly as he told of the girl's screams coming from inside the shack, that then fell silent. Hours later, Victor had emerged with the big book he carried with him under his arm, and his eyes now with a triumphant glint. Thankfully, his stay ended soon after, and he disappeared down the road out of the village.

"If only we had the courage then to have set that shack on fire with man and monster both inside, and free ourselves," Vlad the key holder had lamented. "I don't know how many years have passed," he said, "but now, it seems as if we are as much the prisoners of our children's murderer as we imprison it." He showed Bela the cross that marked the grave of the mongoloid girl the nosferatu had killed. She had died an innocent, but they took no chances, burying her face down with a stake driven through her body to keep her pinned down in the grave.

Bela had convinced the man to let him see the creature, certain he would find some pathetic, insane outcast the locals had blamed for the loss of their young ones taken by disease. But when the door had been unlocked and opened, all certainty he ever had of how the shadowed folk tales of his ancestors would disappear with the light of the modern age vanished forever. His first thought had been that the limbless torso laying in the shadowed corner opposite of the hearth fire had been dead and mumified for a long while. That had been till Vlad the key holder walked past the flames to kick the thing in it's ribcage, with an order to look alive. That was when it hissed, and wriggled away across the dirt floor from it's tormentor. Bela had only been able to stare with speechless disbelief at the thing, as the key holder walked out the door with a look of disgust.

"You are Victor's brother," came the phlegmy hiss as the limbless thing fought to sit up against the wall, halfseen through the darkness in the dancing firelight. The chain fastened to the iron ring around it's neck, binding it to a post at the far back wall, rattled as it moved. "I can smell your kindred blood on you." In the half light, Bela could see the dried blood on it's mouth, and how it's belly had bloated outward. Following his eyes, a grin appeared on the creature's skull like face. "Victor lived up to his promise. I haven't fed so well for a long time." Bela realized it's swollen stomach had to have been filled with blood of the girl from the last town. He had to look away as a wave of nausea and disgust swept over him, when it asked: "What is it you want from me?"

"Why... did my brother come to you?" Bela had managed to ask, feeling a numbness come over him that should have been terror. He only then realized how his whole body had trembled.

The nosferatu's laughter was a sibilant, hacking cough. "Surely you know! He told me how he lived with a fear of dying as miserably as your father had. Already, he was feeling the pain in his stomach, and saw the blood in his shit. He thinks life of any kind is better than an end like that!" Again came that hideous laugh. "So much so, that he asked for a vile of my blood."

"To what end?" Bela had asked, dropping to one knee to look into the shriveled, blackened eyes deep inside it's eyelids. He could see the blackened marrow of severed bone in the stumps where limbs had once been. "What did he want your blood for?"

"He wants to drink it and be like me, and live forever!" it laughed gleefully. "He wants to be of the undead!"

Bela had run out of the shack, and slammed the door shut, but still heard the nosferatu's laughter from within. Wiping his tearing eyes, he found the key holder had waited outside for him, his face downcast with grief and shame. Bela told the man that keeping that monster alive wasn't punishing it, as he had been right that the whole village had become prisoners of the demon they had kept locked away. "Burn the shack to the ground, like you wanted to," he told gray bearded Vlad, "and be rid of that godless thing."

***

The story Bela told me over lunch that day ended with his tears. Tears for vainly trying to save his brother, only to learn what a monster he was and probably always had been. And tears for the simple, mongoloid girl who her neighbors had denied humanity to, first as they demeaningly used her as a prostitute, then sold her to Victor as if she was just a lifeless thing. Bela had never known her in life, but he thought she probably never had a single day of happiness, and had died in unimaginable horror so that his brother could damn himself. Wiping his wet face with his napkin, he said he hoped the girl's village had damned themselves for what they had done to her, too. He only prayed the poor girl, whose name he had never learned, had finally found peace. As Bela knew what it was like to be an outcast, himself, I think he let his heart break for that lost innocent.

"But the whole story…, about that… creature," I remember whispering as I took his hand from across the table, "it can't possibly be true… can it?" The sunny sky above the cafe patio might as well have darkened as my mood had been filled with growing dread.

"I saw it with my own eyes," he choked out with hurried desperation, his face ghost white. "Everything we thought were only stories we listened to the old people tell… they're all real. Somehow terribly real! Since then, I avoid the counryside for the city as much as I can, because I think such beings stay in the quiet places where few people are. And even in the city, I try to avoid staying out after dark as much as I can." His eyes had become saucer wide as his whole body shook.

It was only with someone's laughter that Bela fell silent. Looking around we found the other diners in their fine clothes either were looking at him with sneers of ridicule and contempt, or had warily gotten up and moved to tables further away from us, muttering between themselves while they eycd him with scorn.

"I'm sorry… So sorry," he had mumbled as he stood and tried to regain his composure. Without another word, he had walked away, leaving his food unfinished. I never saw him again, and my letters to him went unanswered.

Chapter XI

We all sat in silence, night having fallen outside the house'
windows, as Josie read from the letter's last page out loud:

"It was in the late 1890's, and my husband and I were happily
living our lives in Seattle, when I received news about the Naggy
castle in Hungary. A letter came, written by the property's
caretaker, Gregor Orban, who Victor had left in charge in his
absence. He had informed me that Victor had relocated to America,
in the wilds of Washington state, and that he was having his library
of books, furniture, bags of soil dug up from around the castle
(which made Mr. Orban question the lord's sanity), and the portrait
of himself sent ahead to a property he had purchased in Lincoln
county. The caretaker said he had written specifically to me hoping
I could intervene on behalf of the poor peasants who had worked the
fields, maintaining Victor's wealth, who were all being evicted now
that the castle and the rest of the property were being sold.

"Mr. Orban had earlier on appealed to Victor's older brother,
Bela in Berlin, only to be told that he had been estranged from
Victor for years. He asked the caretaker not to write him again. As
the only other living Naggy relative he knew of, he thought I might
be able to intervene, as his own letters to Victor, who hadn't been

back to the castle for years now, had returned from America unopened.

"I told Mr. Orban I'd do what I could. Writing to Victor, I reintroduced myself as his cousin who had spent over half a year of my long past childhood with his brother and him at the castle, and appealed to him to show sympathy for those villagers who had nowhere else to go. My letter came back from the other side of the Cascades, also unopened.

"My husband David had asked if I wanted to pay my cousin a visit, and appeal to his better angels face-to-face. After all, David had retired and we had plenty of money to enjoy travel. I told him, no. I don't know how much of Bela's story was true. None of it? Some of it? Maybe all of it? I had considered the possibility that Bela's tale had been the work of a disturbed mind, as it was too terrible to be true. And every time, I came back to the same conclusion that as rattled and frightened as Bela had been when we last met, he was still perfectly sane. I didn't want to go to visit Victor, for fear of what I might find."

Looking up as she shuffled the pages in her hands, Josie said, "I won't bore you with the social niceties Mrs. Phelps ended her letter with." Her eyes moved again across our expressionless faces before she spoke again. "I am aware how the story she told sounds like something ghoulish written by the likes of Edgar Allan Poe. But as unbelievable as it all sounds, what's undeniable is that our animals have been slaughtered by something that doesn't seem to be man or wild beast. It's undeniable what I saw... try to get into my room last night," her voice cracked, and she had to pause for a moment. Looking directly at me, her eyes kind, she said softly, "And what Joe saw as a boy, in this very house, can not any longer be denied, either."

I felt a hand jostle my shoulder, gently. It was Mr. Kahl. The other faces around me turned and nodded. I had been Foggy Headed Joe since that night when I had been twelve. I realized, for the first time, all such thoughts about me – at least in this room - had vanished.

"Well, I'm still for killing the Goddamn thing, now more than ever." Gary said, as he stood up with a resolute expression on his dark face. He clenched his jaw tightly and looked at the rest of us about the room.

Mr. Kahl on the couch beside me stood up as well. "I didn't want to believe any of this was even possible. It's still hard for me to..." Shaking his head, he clasped his hands contritely in both his hands. "But whether I want to believe or not, I should've never doubted my girl."

Josie said something to him quietly in German, which caused him to raise his face to her with tears in his eyes. "Danke, Liebschen." He nodded with a gratified smile.

McMurty raised his hand slowly. "Uh… Josie?"

"Yes?"

"Uh… that word Mrs. Phelps kept using...," he asked, his normally bullish manner now subdued. "Nosferatu…. What exactly is that?"

"It's a Slavic word. It means vampire."

***

The sun rising behind us threw our five shadows across the ground before us, as it did the badly mortared building we stood in front of, after a mostly sleepless night huddled together in the Kahl house. It was in this badly constructed building we all agreed would be the first place where we should look for Nagy. Mr. Kahl, Gary, and I held our rifles lowered to the ground, while McMurty held a sledge hammer by it's handle with both hands at waist level. We had talked about getting dynamite from town to blow up the brick building, till the big cowboy said he'd sooner knock the door down. Josie, having changed her dress from last night into her overalls and work shirt, laid a hand on the small of my back. A lantern, it's light burning weakly in the sunlight, hung half forgotten in her other hand.

"Josie, you don't have to be here," Mr. Kahl said.

"I do," she said, her voice solemn. "I want to see this to the end."

"McMurty," Mr. Kahl gestured to the door, "pound away."

Hefting the handle with both hands with a grunt, McMurty swung the hammer with all the power in his muscular arms and shoulders. The crash of the iron hammer head splintering the wooden door carried in the air across the empty scabland. Taking a deep breath, he reared the hammer back and swung again. And again. And again, till the hammer smashed a hole through the wood.

Resting the hammer's head on the ground, McMurty leaned with exhaustion on the handle as sweat rolled down his face. "Oak, Goddamn it," he panted. "It had to be oak." He pulled his hat off from his sweaty hair, despite the cool of the morning.

When nobody else moved for that moment, I stepped forward to the splintered hole in the door, and resting my gun against the poorly constructed wall, I looked into the blackness inside. I felt my heart pounding behind my ribs. "Could I have some light?"

With Josie having stepped forward to hand me the lantern, I raised in front of me and felt it's heat against my face as I looked inside, and reported what little I saw in the yellowing light. "I can see a pile of books… and what looks like a hole in the ground." Then I reached inside.

"Joe, don't," I heard Josie gasp from behind me.

Squeezing my eyes shut, I felt faint as I slid my hand inside the gaping hole, half expecting something to grab my hand on the other side of the door. *Why am I doing this???* my mind screamed at me. *Because I want to see this to the end, just like Josie said,* I answered myself. I did it for me now, and for the boy I had been whose life had been ruined years before. Feeling around inside, my hand touched the squared edges of a piece of wood against the otherside of the door, set in what felt like metal brackets. Turning my head, I said, "I think I found a bar holding the door."

"Can you lift it?" Mr. Kahl asked.

I shook my head. "I think the hole has to be bigger."

"Goddamn it," McMurty grumbled with a shake of his head as he walked up behind me, lifting the hammer over his shoulder, again. "Well, get out of the way." Feeling the splinters tug at my shirt sleeve as I pulled my arm out of the hole, I moved aside for him. "Goddamn oak!" he roared as he smashed through more of the door with a couple more blows.

I raised a hand for him to stop. "I think that's big enough."

"Better be." Gasping for breath, McMurty dropped the hammer to lean with a hand against the wall's jutting brick work for support. Putting my hand inside the enlarged hole, I took hold of the door's bar, and grunting with effort, I awkwardly lifted it till I was able to push it to the side of the doorframe, and heard it thunk on the ground. Mr. Kahl and Gary approached, rifles at the ready, when I pulled on the hole in the door. It opened outward with a creak of long unused hinges to the darkness within.

McMurty's eyes widened. "How the holy hell did anybody bar the door from the inside?" he exclaimed, seeing the iron brackets for the wooden bolt fastened to the inside of the door. "There isn't even a door handle on the outside!"

I warily stepped inside with the lantern held in front of me, and instantly breathed in the unpleasant, earthy smell I could taste in my mouth. There, inside were beams of wood leaning haphazardly against the mortared brick wall and ceiling, as if some ameteur builder had hurried the work along. Or perhaps his work had been so poor that it came close to collapsing before the mortar dried. "Mein Gott," whispered Mr. Kahl with astonishment from behind me, at the sight of the large hole in the middle of the dirt floor, from which a protruding ladder led down into blackness. "Where does that lead to?"

Josie's shadow blocked out the feeble sunlight outside when she peered in the doorway. "What are those books against the wall?" she asked. "Can you see well enough to read anything from them?"

Stepping cautiously around the hole in the ground, I knelt down on a knee to examine the carelessly pile of ancient, worm eaten books in the light from the lamp I set down beside me. Nearby on the ground was a candle holder, it's candle burned down to puddled wax. Opening the faded cover of one, I flipped through the yellowed, brittle pages, unable to read the Non-English script. There, I saw unsettling illustrations on some pages of skeletal looking men laying inside coffins within mortuaries. Then of the creatures walking under a starry night. And of it climbing through an open window while a woman slept under the covers of her bed. I felt a chill. Somehow, the tiny space felt as if it had grown smaller, and the air seemed harder to breathe. Looking at another, I found the same. "I can't read what language it's in." I shook my head, and wiped at my brow, finding it sweaty despite how cool it was inside.

Something on the ground gleamed in the light. It was a glass vial laying beyond the books. Picking it up, I saw what I took to be flakes of dried blood inside. Remembering Mrs. Phelps' letter recount how Victor Nagy had made a deal with the limbless vampire to gain a vile of it's blood to drink, I quickly threw it away with disgust. Without warning, I became all too aware of the tight space where I was; of the brick walls that seemed to close in on me, and how the gaping shaft in the earthen floor seemed to widen, leaving me with less and less solid space.

Shaking my head, I rubbed my eyes. "I need to get out of here," I called out, even as my lungs threatened to stop sucking in air.

"Are you alright, Joseph?" Mr. Kahl asked as I blundered past him into the clean morning sunlight.

Nodding as I struggled to gasp in lungful after lungful of air, I managed to say, "I just need to breathe… just need to breathe." When my knees threatened to give way and let me fall, Josie held me up with her arms tightly around me, no longer caring to hide affection she felt for me from her father. My heartbeat was starting to slow as I returned her embrace, when I looked at my empty hands over her shoulder, and realized I had left the lantern inside. Closing my eyes tightly with shame, I thought: *Oh God, I'm such a pathetic coward, and everyone sees it.*

I overheard Gary and Mr. Kahl talk about climbing down the ladder into the hole.

Taking a deep breath, I closed my eyes. "I'll go with you," I called to them, feeling the world reel abound me. I might have fallen if Josie hadn't still been holding me.

"No, you're not," she said softly into my ear. "Let my dad and the others do it."

"I have to," I whispered, my throat dust dry, as I turned from her, my fingers slipping from her hand.

"You don't have to prove anything to me, Joe."

"I've got something to prove to myself," I said, thinking I had to do this for the twelve year old boy I used to be as well, as I picked up my rifle I had left leaning against the brick wall.

Mr. Kahl and McMurty went inside the building already, guns at the ready, as Gary climbed down the ladder, lantern in hand, when he started shouting in the Salish language of his Spokane tribe.

"We can't understand you, Gary!" Mr. Kahl yelled back with concern. "Say it in English."

"There's a graveyard down here!"

McMurty was already following Mr. Kahl down the ladder into the glow of lamp light below, when I stepped inside. I climbed down to the three men standing in shocked silence within a narrow, earthen walled passageway, held up with timber support beams. There, in the light and shadow, I found myself looking between the heads and shoulders of the men in front of me, much as I had as a boy when my pa took me to see the corpse of the outlaw, Harry Tracy, on display in Davenport for the crowds of locals. Numb, my mouth fell open as my eyes took in the pile of human bones dressed in torn, rotting clothing spread out in the tunnel space into the dark beyond sight. Among the jumble of human skulls, rib cages, and long bones was one skeleton dressed in a plaid work shirt, checkered pants, and with a revolver uselessly still holstered at it's belt. I recognized that as the drifter I had wanted to spook for the sake of childish revenge all those years before.

Why couldn't I have just imagined it all? Why did it have to be real? The voice of the twelve year old I had once been sobbed inside my head, as I felt fear squeeze my heart.

Mr. Kahl broke the silence, his eyes remaining on the human bones. "McMurty, could you roll me a cigarette?" Without a word, the big cowboy did as asked, never once caring to ask when Mr. Kahl had taken up smoking. Striking a match against a wooden beam, he lit Mr. Kahl up. "Thank you, much," Mr. Kahl said tonelessly.

"Dad? Joe?" Josie hollered from above the hole, where her face was a shadow over the ladder. "What's happening?"

"Liebschen… please go back to the house," Mr. Kahl answered back, attempting to keep his voice steady. "I'll tell you everything. I promise."

"It's alright, Josie," I said, before she reluctantly left the hole above the earthen passage. After I was certain she had left, I told Mr. Kahl, "Myself, I think your daughter would be the last person I know to turn yellow and run at this sight," motioning to the human remains that must have taken years accumulate into the piles strewn down the passageway.

He nodded sadly. "That's what I'm afraid of. She has too much of her mother's heart." Turning to the darkness ahead of us, he said, "Let's see where this goes."

As the four of us walked ahead, the light from the lamp pushing the blackness away from the earthen walls, Mr. Kahl said, "When this is all over with, I'm going to fill this whole Goddamn thing up with dirt."

***

Another ladder rising into a hole in the ceiling appeared maybe a hundred yards further, when the tunnel ended at a wall. Looking up the ladder in the lantern light, Gary said, "Something's covering the top. It looks like wood."

"Hold the light up for me," I said, then ungainly climbed up the rungs to the top with my rifle in one hand, till that wooden covering was above my head. Was I scared? I could easily have shit my pants if I hadn't used the privy before heading out to the brick building earlier that morning. But as I said, I needed to see this thing through. My pulse beating in my ears for fear of what might be waiting for me above, I pushed the barrel of my rifle against the wooden slab overhead, taken by surprise how easily it moved. I pushed it all the way from the hole's opening with my gun, saying, "I think it's just a piece of plywood." Above me was pitch blackness.

"What do you see?" McMurty asked.

"I don't know. I need light." I handed my rifle down to McMurty's waiting hands, and took the lantern offered by Gary. Closing my eyes and breathing deeply the stale air smelling of dirt, I willed myself to climb the rest of the way up for my head to emerge from the hole.

"Well, what do you see now?" It was McMurty, again.

Holding the lantern high, I looked about me, seeing walls constructed of wooden boards set on a concrete foundation, and row after row of support trellises across the space, holding up a low ceiling was also made of planks. "I… don't know where I am," I said, recounting everything I saw. Climbing all the way out, I crawled on my knees and one hand along the dirt floor, stopping only to swat away at webs alive with spiders along with their cocooned insect prey. Then I saw it, beyond the lamp's glow; sunlight shone narrowly between the wooden boards.

"I think we're above ground," I called out behind me, seeing McMurty coming up out of the hole, followed by Gary. Crawling towards to feeble light from outside, I soon after found the opening of a shaft at one end, running above into the low-level ceiling. Holding the lantern close, I looked upward, and saw the series of handholds along the wall that disappeared into the darkness above.

"I know exactly where we are," I heard Mr. Kahl say, gravely. Turning my head, I saw him sitting splayed legged on the dirt floor in the lantern's yellow light, panting for breath after having climbed up out of the hole, himself. *We're in the crawlspace under my house.*

Chapter XII

"It's been inside the house, probably this whole time," Mr. Kahl told Josie, finishing the story of what we had found in the tunnel beneath the brick building, and how that tunnel led to beneath their home. The warm summer air took on a chill for me as I listened to him recount to his daughter all that we had seen, while the gleaming sun overhead in the cloudless blue sky seemed to lose it's brightness as the three of us stood outside the house. From the other side of the house, we could hear Gary and McMurty tearing siding and boards off from above the foundation to reach the crawlspace inside.

Josie's face had paled as she listened to her father. Her mouth had fallen open, and her eyes widened. "That means… that thing's been listening to us this whole time," she spoke in a hushed tone, despite no longer being inside where prying ears could hear her. "It might have heard me read Mrs. Phelp's letter…. which means it knows it's been found out." She turned her face away and shivered noticeably, despite the late summer heat.

"Yes." Her father nodded. "Which is why I wanted to talk outside."

"But then why hasn't it done anything to stop us, yet?" I asked.

"As I recall my folklore," Josie said, after breathing in deeply to regain some composure, "I believe vampires can only come out at night. They supposedly avoid sunlight at all cost. But tonight..." Her voice trailed off, again appearing to be shaken.

"How much can we depend on folk tales, though?" Mr. Kahl gestured with his open hands as he spoke. "Until last night, I wouldn't believe I'd even be asking about this!" he said more to himself than to us, looking up at the sky with an exasperated shake of his head.

"Until last night, dad, I doubt any of us believed in Vampires. Folk tales are all we have to rely on." Looking between the two of us, she asked, "Which begs the question… what do we do now? From the work you've put McMurty and Gary to, we're obviously staying to fight, right? We're not running away before sundown."

"I sunk everything I have in this place," Mr. Kahl gently took hold of his daughter's upper arms as he spoke. "I thought my life was over after I lost your mother, but then I came here for the two of us to start over, again. I'm not going to let some monster that should only exist in that *Dracula* book take it all from me. Short of setting the house on fire, the only alternative we have is to follow that secret`passage Joe here found inside the wall to where ever it leads," he said, his eyes moving from the bottom floor to the third at the top, "and hopefully get the jump on that thing while it's still sleeping."

"Tell us what to do, Mr. Kahl," I said, "and we'll follow you to the letter."

"Alright, I've got an important job for you." He laid a fatherly hand on my shoulder.

"Anything."

"I need you to hitch up the wagon, and take Josie away to Davenport."

"What? I'm not going anywhere!" She turned to face her father, eyes blazing.

"I was ready to die when I lost your mother." He shook his head. "I'm not going to risk losing you, now."

"And if you do this alone, I'll lose you! This is my home as much as it's yours, and I'll fight to keep it, too!"

"Providing that those two boys will stay and give me a hand, I won't be alone." Mr. Kahl turned his face to me. "Joe? You're the only other person in the world she'd leave here for."

He knew, then, I realized, how Josie and I felt about one another. But now was hardly the time for pressing him to express acceptance or disapproval of it all.

"Joe… please, no..." Her eyes tearing, she begged me not to obey her father this time.

I took a deep breath before speaking. "Josie, I'm sorry, but your dad loves you," I could only mumble. I knew at that moment I risked her hating me, forever.

Curling her hands into fists, she started hitting her father as she shouted at him in German, tears streaming down her face. Grabbing her by her wrists, he roared back at her in German, his face turning red with fury, causing her to shrink back from him. Releasing her hands that looked so tiny in his, he pointed at the barn, and gruffly snapped at her. Turning, she wiped her eyes and walked with her head bowed in resignation to the the barn's open doorway.

I dropped my own eyes to the ground, feeling uneasy for witnessing the argument that had ended as quickly as it had begun. Mr. Kahl gently laid a hand on my shoulder, and said, "I'll ask one of the other boys to help you with the wagon," his voice trembling as if near to tears himself.

***

For the whole ride to Davenport, Josie had sat without speaking to me on her side of the buckboard seat, eyes directed straight ahead with a frown mixed with anger and heartache on her face. With the horses reigns in my hands, I had tried explaining to her why I hadn't disobeyed her father. I had stammered on about how I wished Mr. Kahl had been my father, as my own had come to regard me as a waste after I first laid eyes on the thing haunting her house. That her father had been the only other person, outside herself, to take a chance that I wasn't the sick-in-the-head-liar like everyone else around here thought I was, and that I owed him for that. And of

course, that I was also concerned with her well being. But it all just
rambled out of my mouth as so much nonsense. We men really
don't know anything about baring our hearts and souls, even when
we want to. Goddamn it all.

The only thing she said, turning to me, was: "I'm going to hate
you for the rest of my life."

The horses had moved listlessly down the road, as if they had just
been worked so hard that they were at the point of dropping. No
amont of cracking the reigns on my part made them trot any faster.
By the time we reached Davenport, dusk had already fallen, with the
sun just a glow on the horizon. Street lights had already turned on.
Mr. Kahl had given me money to house the horses in the livery
stable, as well as enough for something to eat, and lodgings for the
night. He had given me a stern look, and said, "Be sure to rent two
different rooms." I had nodded quickly, promising we'd be sleeping
in two different beds. He also had asked me to call when we got to
town, after settling in.

At the diner where I ordered dinner for us, Josie had sat across
the table from me, arms crossed and with a sullen look on her face.
When I asked her what she'd like to eat, she only muttered, "I'm not
hungry." As famished as I was, I knew she wasn't telling the truth.
When the waitress came by, I ordered the steak and eggs for the two
of us. Excusing myself, I stood up from my chair, and walked past
the few townsfolk, farmers, and ranchers seated around me over to
the service counter, where I asked if I could make a call. The fry
cook let me use the telephone in the office.

The Davenport switchboard operator connected me to the Kahl
residence. I was surprised when McMurty answered over the
receiver I held to my ear: "Hello? Can you hear me? I can't figure
out this damn, newfangled thing!"

"It's me, McMurty! I can hear you perfectly fine," I spoke loudly
over him into the receiver. "Can I talk to Mr. Kahl?"

"The boss is asleep. He's totally bushed after climbing all the
way up that shaft inside the wall."

"He did it all by his lonesome?"

"He sure did, even though Gary and me offered to go, ourselves.
But he said it was his house, and he should have been taking the
risks, himself, as only one person at a time could fit. He climbed all

the way up to an attic above Josie's room, carrying the lantern in one hand. Shit, that would just about tucker out a fella our age!"

I could understand why he hadn't wanted his daughter present, as he had been intending to risk his own safety climbing up into the darkness of that shaft, having no idea what might be waiting for him.

"What did he find?"

"You aren't going to believe this, Joe. He discovered that passage opened up to a secret door inside a closet on every floor. That includes Josie's room! He said he found weird symbols drawn all over the attic walls in chalk, along with dirt spread out on the floor."

"Dirt?" My brow furrowed with surprise.

"Yeah. The boss says it looked like someone's been lying in it."

Immediately, I recalled the other day when Josie and I had heard something scratching above her ceiling, and the two of us thinking it only a rodent. The small attic door near the roof also floated through my mind, making me realize how easily it could have clambered down to the balcony outside her room, and taken her at any time it wanted to.

"What about the..." I stopped speaking to look about and seeing no one, I asked, "What about the vampire?" Even alone in the office, I kept my voice low.

"The attic was empty." I could imagine McMurty shrugging. "The boss thinks whoever or whatever was there must have flown the coop, already."

Telling McMurty I'd call again tomorrow, I hung up and returned to the table. Recounting everything McMurty told me, I saw Josie's face pale at the knowledge that a monster was literally above her as she slept. Regaining her calm, she reached over the table for my hand, and smiled contritely. "Joe, I'm sorry for what I said. I could never hate you. I was just so out of sorts about my dad. The thought of leaving him..."

"I know." I nodded, gently squeezed her hand in mine.

After our dinner was served and we ate, I asked, "What about the dirt?" shaking my head in puzzlement. "Any answers in folklore about that?"

Between bites of meat and scrambled egg she had stabbed on her fork, she said, "A vampire supposedly needs to sleep in it's native soil." When a burly farmer at the next table snickered, having overheard her, she stared him down a dirty look. Turning back to me, she now lowered her voice to almost a whisper: "That begs the question, if it wasn't asleep in the attic… where did it go?"

***

The knock on my hotel room door awakened me. "Hold your horses!" I called out, sleepily, before I sat up and swung my feet out of bed to the floor. Finding my way through the darkness, I opened the door to a small, older man with long hair hanging out from under his hat. Yeah?" I asked, blinking my eyes in the hallway's light. It took a moment to shake the cobwebs from my head to recognize him as the attendant at the livery stable.

"Sir, the two horses you brought in this evening look pretty sick. I normally wouldn't bother you at this hour, but neither of them look like they can stand up much longer. I'm sorry, but I can't risk the other animals getting sick from them."

"Wait… what…?" I shook my head, still feeling more asleep than awake. "Let me get my clothes on, and I'll take a look."

***

Turning on the electric lights in the stable, the attendant led the way to the two stalls next to each other, where I had quartered the horses. There, I saw how one was swaying back and forth in the narrow space, as if drunk. The other had already fallen to the straw covered floor.

"Let me take a look," I said. I recalled how sluggishly both horses had ridden to town. The attendant unlatched the second door, and let me inside the stall of the horses lying on it's side. Kneeling down beside the animal, I whispered, "It's alright boy," as I stroked his long head. "It's alright." And then I saw it: the bite mark on the side of it's neck, partially obscured by it's mane. "My God," I muttered as I stood up and told the attendant to open the other stall. Inside, I tried to steady the horse as it weaved about on it's hooves while I searched his neck for another bite. Blood had dried on the teeth marks around his throat. No, the horses weren't sick, they had been drained of too much blood.

"I'm sorry, but like I said, I can't let..."

"Do you have a telephone?" I asked, walking out of the stall.

"Yeah…," he nodded with a look of confusion. "It's behind the desk out front."

I heard him call after me as I ran to the front desk, "The switch board operators don't care to have anyone waking them up this late at night. And what am I supposed to do with your sick animals?"

Soon afteward, I was on the stable's telephone, when I heard the operator sleepily grumble if I knew what time it was. Demanding he connect me with the Kahl residence, I stood there for what seemed like an eternity, listening to the ringing through the earpiece.

Pick up, Mr. Kahl, I begged in silent deperation, through that endless ringing. *Anyone, pick up!*

Hanging up with a sense of desperation several minutes later, I hurried back to the stable attendant, who stood by the stall doors, opening up a pouch of chewing tobacco.

"Look sir, I need you to remove your sick animals."

"I need fresh horses hitched up to the buckboard, now," I told him, ignoring his concern about the two horses. "And yes, it's a matter of life and death!"

***

"Josie! Josie!" Frantic, I hammered my fist against her room's door. No one had answered the phone, no matter how many minutes I had waited through that damn ringing.

The door opened a crack to one of her sleepy eyes peering out at me. "Joe? What time is it?" She yawned.

"I don't know," I said, hurriedly, shaking my head. "We have to get back to your father's house, and warn everyone."

"Why? What's happened?" She looked confused with drowsiness.

"You were right; it was listening to us all along. It wasn't in the house, anymore, when your dad was searching for it. It must have been hiding in the barn!"

Chapter XIII

Crickets chirped in the early morning dark when we arrived back at the farm. The waning moonlight was bright enough for us to make out the dim shapes of the farm buildings, while in the west, the dawn shined meagerly along the horizon. The door to the bunk house stood open, and the Kahl house was dark, save for light shining through a third story rear window that was partially visible from the road. "That's my bedroom!" Josie said, keeping her voice low. She turned to me with a stunned expression.

I nodded. "Hand me the lantern," I whispered back. Striking a match to light the lantern, I stepped down from the wagon, and took my rifle out from under the seat. Walking to the open bunk house, I peered inside with the gas light throwing light inside. "Christ on a cross," I swore, turning away too slow not to see the dead man hanging headfirst, halfway off one of the top bunks. Bloody entrails draped over his torso and face from his ripped open stomach. His red stained hands hung uselessly above the floor. I knew he had lived long enough to try stuffing his innards back inside his body.

"What is it?" Josie leaped out of her side of the buckboard, and rushed to me. "Joe, tell me!"

"Josie, don't look," I choked out, quickly putting down my gun to hug her tightly to me with my free arm. "It's a dead body, Josie. You don't want to see."

"Is it my dad?" I could feel her heart suddenly thudding against my body. "I have to see!" She fought to pull away from me.

"It's not, it's not," I assured her. "I think it's Gary." It was from the Spokane Indian's bunk bed that the mutilated body hung from, I realized, as a sob escaped from my mouth. My friend, who had worked beside me all these months, had died more terribly than I could imagine. "Trust me, it's best not to look."

"Was there anyone else in there?" she asked breathlessly.

"I… I don't know," I answered truthfully, shaking my head. "When I saw… I turned away as fast as I could," I admitted.

"Please, I have to know if my dad's in there."

"I'll look, again," I promised her. Steeling myself, I held the lantern up, and with a grimace on my face, looked inside. My stomach threatened to chuck up the steak, eggs, and coffee I had had for dinner earlier in Davenport as I made myself to look with tear blurred eyes on the bloodstained intestines glistening in the light, and the now drying blood that had drenched Gary's mattress and the other in the bunk below, as well as the floor and everything else in sight within the narrow building. The blood was fresh, maybe having been spilled an hour ago, maybe just minutes.

Turning from the doorway, I shook my head and wiped my eyes. "No, I don't see anyone else."

A wailing shrill, long and drawn out, the likes I had never heard before, from inside the house, made our heads whip around.

"What was that?" Josie turned to me with eyes saucer wide. I knew her blood had been as chilled as mine at the sound.

"I don't know," I said, grabbing my rifle and running to the house. "Stay here," I shouted over my shoulder to her, only to see her following after me.

"The hell I will!"

Only then did I realize that the front door was open, and blood was all over the handle. "Take this," I said, handing the lantern to Josie. "Stay close so I have light." I cocked the rifle and held it's butt up to my shoulder and my finger on the trigger, before walking into the darkened house. My heart pounding, I took in the broken furniture tossed haphazardly about the room in the lantern's glow close behind me. I could hear Josie's ragged breath come close to sobbing. "It's okay," I said soothingly to her, all the while keeping my eyes straight ahead.

"Look, on the floor," she whispered, nasally with tears. There was a trail of blood across the hardwood floor.

That wailing cry came from upstairs, again, but now it was filled with rage, followed by the sound of splintering wood. My hair standing on end, I rushed up the stairs, with the light from Josie's lantern barely able to keep up with my feet as she ran after me.

Stepping onto the third floor, I froze in place as I stared at the thing smashing through the outside of the bedroom door, from where light on the other side poured out of. Josie almost ran into me, when she too stopped, and could only stare from in back of me. Yellowish brown in color, it might as well have been just a skeleton covered with dried, papery hide. Without clothing, I could count the ridges of it's ribs along it's back, as well as the bloodless, tattered exit wounds peppering it's body. Tufts of black hair clung to it's skull.

Taking hold of the splintered door, the creature ripped it off it's hinges with a wheezing grunt, then used the door as a battering ram to strike the bookshelf that had been placed up against it on the inside of the room. Tipping forward, the bookshelf crashed loudly. I could hear voices I recognized as belonging to Mr. Kahl and McMurty crying out fearfully. One of them fired a shot that went wild. Tossing the door aside, the creature stalked into the bedroom, walking over the bookshelf that now laid face down, it's books scattered over the floor.

"Victor Nagy!" Josie called, stepping into the hallway from behind me. "Please, Victor, stop."

The thing did stop at her voice. A heartbeat or two later, it turned around, slowly. It's face was shriveled, with a hole in the middle where a nose should have been, while the eyesockets looked empty with shadow. Sparse hair clung to it's chin, and it's arms were painted with wet and drying blood past it's elbows. This was the creature I had seen murder that drifter all those years ago, and left my life in ruins. It wasn't a chill I felt; I was ice cold. And then it spoke, but the words from it's creaking voice weren't English.

"We can't understand you, Victor," Josie kept her voice steady as she inched forward till she was moving past me. "Can you speak English?"

"I said.. I haven't been called by that name since a lifetime ago." The whispery sounds it spoke with left me unnerved. But there was also something almost sorrowful about it. "This is my house. You've been trespassing here for months."

I aimed my rifle, but Josie had stepped ahead of me, too close to my line of fire. "Josie, get out of the way," I muttered between clenched teeth, hearing my blood hammer in my ears.

"Alright, this is your house," She said, as she raised her hands open palmed. "Dad?" she called out, craning her neck to look into the open doorway. Are you there?"

"I'm here," her father called back, weakly. "McMurty's badly hurt."

"Listen, Victor, please just let me take my father and the other man, and we'll go."

"But who says I want any of you to go? I'd be left to starve!"
Nagy's laughter was a phlegmy rasp as it's lips split into a smile of
blackened, sharpened teeth. "Now you all get to die."

"Get away from her!" Mr. Kahl, stripped down to his long johns,
appeared in the doorway behind the skeletal thing, the revolver in his
hand firing. Nagy shuddered for a moment, then shook his head
with a chuckle.

"Do you think this is the first time I've been shot, German?"

Faster than a shocked Mr. Kahl could pull the trigger, Nagy had
his wrist in his hand, twisting the gun up at the ceiling, when it fired,
again. Nagy's treasured dirt spilled to the floor from the bullet hole
from the attic. "I don't remember how pain is supposed to feel
anymore," the vampire sneered, when he drove his boney fingers
into Mr. Kahl's belly, and up under his ribcage. "But I know you
do."

"Dad!" Josie screamed, both hands pressed to either side of her
face, as we watched as Nagy lifted her father with one hand into the
air, his face a tortured mask of pain, then threw him across the room.
We heard the glass paned doors shatter.

"Josie, get out of the way!"

She threw herself against the wall I roared before I squeezed the
trigger. The rifle's deafening report sent Nagy sprawling face
forward with a spray of bloodless debris from his chest. Cocking my
rifle again, I stepped through the doorway and over the downed
bookshelf. Sweeping my eyes across the room, I saw Mr. Kahl
laying outside on the balcony, amid broken glass and wood.
McMurty laid stirring on the bed, the covers bloodstained like his
long johns, with his hands pressed against the red ruin of his face.

Unsteadily pushing himself up from the books scattered about the
floor, Nagy turned around as he regarded the broken ribs visible in
the gaping hole I had made in his chest. For a scant second, I
thought I could see the bedroom's back wall through the exit wound.
Rifle butt at my shoulder, again, I took aim with my teeth bared in
rage – for the woman I loved, for my friends he hurt and killed, for
ruining my life eight years ago - when he looked at me and grinned
unexpectedly.

"I know you," he giggled, pointing at me. "I haven't seen you
since you were a boy!" He began sauntering toward me, knowing he

saw how the blood ran from my face. "I always thought, you were
the one who got away. I wouldn't have imagined you'd come back
and give me a second chance."

I pulled the trigger again, blasting a hole in the far wall in an
explosion of plaster fragments and dust, a split second after Nagy
ducked lightening quick out of the way. And then in a blink of an
eye, I was on the floor with the wind knocked out of my lungs
beneath the creature's weight, his knees pressing the rifle gripped in
my hands against my chest.

He leaned over me, his face inches from mine. "I'm going to rip
your head half off, and drink the blood spraying out of your neck!"
Curling his lips back from those discolored, dagger like teeth, his
mouth spread wide open as he pushed my head back. Grimacing, the
stench of rotted flesh from that breathless mouth made my stomach
churn, as I prayed it would be quick.

"Get away from him, or I'll set this whole house on fire!" I heard
Josie's angry voice. "I'll burn it all, including your precious soil in
the attic."

After the vampire stood up from me, I struggled to sit up as I saw
her holding the lantern glowing brightly in her outstretched hand
over the books scattered about her feet..

"Oh, you aren't going to do that," Nagy hissed, grabbing the rifle
deliberately from my numbed fingers, and snapped the barrel like a
twig, before tossing it aside. Dropping to all fours, he crawled
toward her, looking like a giant, emaciated spider. His voice rattled,
"The living so want to avoid pain; especially the sort that comes with
burning to death. You want to avoid death, even more."

"You want to risk that?" She raised the lantern overhead in a
motion to dash it to the floor.

"No." He became motionless.

"My original offer still stands." Her voice had begun shaking
with emotion, but her face remained stolidly calm. "Let us go, and
we'll leave you in peace." Her eyes still on Nagy, she choked out,
"Joe… please check on my dad," as tears ran down her face.

I stood up slowly, feeling pain from being wrestled to the floor by
a monster. The vampire turned his head for his gaze to follow me as
I limped slowly to the balcony.

Stepping out into the early morning darkness, I knelt down next to Mr. Kahl, despite the broken glass under my knees. My eyes were on the horrible wound in his stomach that soaked his under shirt with blood, when he moaned and attempted to sit up.

"It's alright, boss," I whispered to him, amazed he was still alive after all this. "I'll get you out of here."

His blue eyes fluttering to stay open in his bloodlessly white face, he shook his head. "It's too late for me… Get Josie and McMurty out of here." I wanted to tell him he was going to be alright, but the words stopped before they came out of my mouth. I nodded, knowing as well as he did that he had little time left.

All the while, I could hear Nagy speaking from inside. "It didn't have to be like this. I wasn't going to kill you people like I did those vagrants and bums."

"Stay where you are," came Josie's angry voice. "I'm warning you."

"I was content living off your livestock. The night I came into your room, I was only going to feed a little, and leave you alive. But you had to start screaming, and left me no choice but to leave out the balcony door. We all could have been happy."

Mr. Kahl's bloody fingers gripped my shirt. "Take care of Josie…," he whispered, blood running from his lips down his chin. "Promise me."

"I promise, I will." Nodding, tears streamed down my face.

Then unexpectedly, he pushed himself up, trembling weakly with pain. "Joseph… help me up." Nodding, I put my arm around his shoulder, and helped him stand up. He gestured to the scene in the bedroom, where the monster, having risen upright, was only feet away from his daughter. "Go get McMurty," he coughed blood. "I'll distract it." That was when Mr. Kahl pushed away from me, and stumbled inside the room, his bowels hanging from the rent in his torso.

"Dad!"

Nagy turned his head to Mr. Kahl, just as he lunged from behind, wrapping his arms around the fiend, and pulling him to the floor. "Throw the lantern, Josie!" he cried. When he saw her hesitate, dumbstruck, he yelled, "I'm already dead! Throw it!"

"Don't!" For the first time, there was fear in Nagy's voice.

Rearing the lantern back over her shoulder, she threw it across the room, where it's glass casing shattered on impact with the floor. Flaming oil spread in all directions.

"I love you liebschen!"

With a scream, the vampire tossed Mr. Kahl off like a rag doll. Rushing to the fire, he dropped down on his knees as he tried patting it out. But the blaze was already climbing the wall and the curtains, lapping at the ceiling and racing to the nearby bookshelves. Soon, he was engulfed in flames. From the bed where I had rushed over to, I saw Nagy stand up to move toward the doorway, his very flesh crumbling in the flames, when Mr. Kahl wrapped his arms around the vampire's legs from the floor, even as his own body burned. Pitching forward with a howl, the vampire landed hard on the floor, his limbs and body shattered like wood burning to embers.

Black smoke billowing through the room, my hands groped blindly around the bed till I found McMurty. Coughing, and my eyes stinging with tears, I pulled on McMurty's arm, to no avail. "Get up, you big bastard!" I slapped McMurty hard, when he started to sit up with a groan. When another pair of unseen hands taking hold of his other arm, the two of us dragged him from the bed. Josie and I stumbled out the bedroom door and down the stairs with McMurty held up between us, smoke filling up the stairwell.

Cold, early morning air never tasted better when we burst out of the house. Coughing and wheezing, the two of us pulled the big man between us to the buckboard wagon. The horses whinnied with fright as fire burst out of the windows and out the door. Black smoke hid the stars above.

Chapter XIV

McMurty was in and out of consciousness when we carried him to the buckboard outside, and took him to the doctor in Davenport, and where Josie and I were treated for smoke inhalation. It was only after that Josie had allowed herself to cry for her father, as I held her tightly. Finding a hotel room, I registered us as Mr. and Mrs. MacReady. She made no objection. I hoped that was a good sign for things to come.

Though McMurty lost a lot of blood along with an eye, the big cowboy pulled through. To his credit, he told the doctors he couldn't remember anything about how he had landed in their care. Visiting him at a hospital in Spokane, where he had been transferred, I found him bedridden with a plate of food he had only picked at.

"You're going to get skinny eating like that," I told him, hoping to get him to laugh after having pulled up a chair next to his bed.

"Not too hungry these days," he said, tonelessly. Even with the bloodstained bandages covering the greater part of his face, I could see how sad he looked. "My head's filled with thoughts these days." He shook his head. "And I'm not used to thinking or mulling things over much."

I couldn't help but laugh. "What are you thinking about?" I asked, even though I damn well knew his head was filled with the same thoughts and memories as mine.

"How are we supposed to make people understand what happened? How are we even supposed to make them believe any of it?" his voice sank to a whisper when he saw a nurse walk past his door. "I don't know if I believe any of it, anymore."

I nodded, leaning forward in my chair, with elbows on my legs, and my hat held in my hands. "Josie and I talked it over, figuring we might tell the world what happened, and get sent to an insane asylum." I shrugged. "Or maybe get accused of concocting a crazy story to cover for murdering Mr. Kahl, and end up going to the gallows, or prison for life. It's bad enough that the county sherrif turned the whole place upside down after we reported the human bones we found in the tunnel. So, we agreed we would just say Victor Nagy, the original owner of the house, was a lunatic who had been hiding right under our noses, after killing scores of people over the years. He had been killing our animals, then one night got into the bunk house, killed Gary and attacked you. And that Mr. Kahl died while fighting off that madman after he got into the house, when a gas lamp got broken, and the whole place went up in flames. We reported Nagy died in the fire, with him."

McMurty sighed. "I guess nobody can say that's a lie."

"As it turns out, I was right. We found dirt mixed in the hay inside the barn, where Nagy was hiding , before we started searching the house. Say, what do you remember happening?"

McMurty said he remembered running from the bunk house, blinded with blood, to Mr. Kahl's front door, crying for help. He visibly shook as he recalled that cadaverous thing following him to the house, when Mr. Kahl had come to his rescue. The boss had pulled him along up the stairs to the safety of Josie's room, firing at that monster to keep it back. McMurty had lain in Josie's bed, dropping into blackness only to awaken again and again, while, Mr.

Kahl had pulled a heavy bookshelf up against the door, then watched the door with his gun in hand. One of the times McMurty had awakened was when the phone endlessly rang downstairs. He remembered Mr. Kahl promising him he was going to get him out of this, and get him to a doctor, before he moved the book shelf back enough to sneak a peek out the door. That had been a terrible mistake, as that thing had been waiting on the otherside probably that whole time. Then he remembered the sound of the door splintering apart.

"I remember you there, and Miss Josie," he said, small voiced, maybe seeing the memories unfolding behind his eyes. "I remember the fire, then you and Miss Josie carrying me down the stairs. Then nothing." He shrugged, eyes cast down at his barely touched plate of food, he muttered, "Every time I close my eyes, I see..." He shook his head as if to clear away the nightmares.

"Do you remember what happened in the bunk house?"

"No…, no," he said quickly with a shake of his head. He sat in silence for a time, his eyes avoiding mine, till he said, "That's not true," his voice low and quaking. Tears rolling down the unbandaged side of his face, his voice cracked "I was supposed to stay awake. It was my turn to stand watch... But I was so tired. I woke up to Gary screaming… screaming!" He shook his head in despair. "It was dark, but I could see it was killing him. And I just ran. It swatted at me when I jumped out of bed and ran past it to the door. It's fingers… it's bony fingers felt like claws down my face. I didn't... help him," he mumbled with shame. Covering his face in his hands, his shoulders rose and fell as he broke down weeping. "Gary was right… I'm a coward."

I didn't know what to say. That he was wrong, that he wasn't a coward, when he finally had to confront himself? I sat quietly till his crying finally stopped.

"I'm sorry," he said, small voiced as he wiped his face. "He was a better man than I'll ever be. I have to go to the Spokane Indian reservation and tell his family. They'll probably think I'm just a crazy white eye," he laughed, sadly.

"That sounds like a good thing to do." I nodded. At least he'd be able to unsaddle himself of that burden he'd otherwise have been carrying around inside, I figured.

"How is Miss Josie?"

"She took her dad's death hard, especially since we had to have a closed casket at the funeral."

"Is she keeping the farm?"

"I don't know," I lied. I knew she could never go back to that place. But her selling the spread and walking away more than likely meant she would leave for a new life, hopefully free from the nightmares threatening to linger with her. I would go with her where ever she went, whether that was to study in Chicago, or to buy a new farm someplace else, I'd be there to take care of her. I had made the promise that I would to the best man I had ever known."

"The nosferatu… the vampire," he asked, now turning his remaining eye to me. "It's dead… The boss killed it, right?"

"Yeah, both Mr. Kahl and Josie killed it." I nodded.

"Is there a body?"

I shook my head. "It burned up in the fire. If anything's left, it's just ash." Reaching over, I jostled his shoulder, affably. "I should get going," I said, rising to my feet. Turning to the door, I said, "Next time I see you, I want you to be eating." I flashed him a smile, and put my hat on. I needed to be back with Josie, and to lose myself in her embrace. When I had left out hotel room in downtown Spokane to visit McMurty, she had busied herself writing to Katarina Phelps in Seattle, to let her know the monster that had once been her cousin was dead. From all evidence of the tunnel filled with the bones of luckless vagrants and drifters, as well as the hiding place in house' attic, she said she would write, Nagy had apparently planned to prey on innocent victims to sustain himself, all along.

The thought came unbidden into my head of that selfish, evil man, sitting naked in that malformed brick building, reciting rituals from his ancient, forbidden books in the dim, flickering fire light, before downing the vial of poisoned vampire blood. He had sought to escape death he was so fearful of, only to become that wretched thing, it's very existence a living death. I forced such chilling thoughts away.

"Joe?"

I turned back to McMurty at the doorway. "Yeah?"

"Do you think there are any others?" I saw the look of uncertainty come over him. It was the same look I had seen in the mirror since that night when I was twelve.

Lowering my head, I closed my eyes, taking in a lungful of air then slowly breathing it out as I searched for an answer. "I don't know," I said finally, with a shake of my head. "Remember Harry Tracy, when he came through this country when we were kids? Do you see any more badmen like him these days? Because I don't. He was maybe the last of that sort of old time desperado; the last of a dying breed. Maybe the same applies to Nagy, too. I think the most we can hope for is, if there are any more like either of them, there probably aren't many left."

"That doesn't make me feel any better." He laughed humorlessly.

"Me neither," I said, before I turned and left.

Bio

Bill Link, or as he was born, William Link Jr., and is a lifelong resident of the Spokane area of Washington State. Thanks to his father, he has been a devoted reader of horror and weird fiction. A graduate of Eastern Washington University, he had earned a Bachelors degree in history, another obsession of his. But it was his love of horror fiction that had led him along the path as a self described starving artist (he says not to let his waist size fool you).

He is the author of anthologies of short stories, entitled, *Creeping Shadows,* and *Your Always With Me And Other Stories*, as well as a novella called, *Skin Like Tanned Leather.* His stories have also, as well as on audio. He is planning to finish another anthology of short fiction. appeared in various collections of fiction. His work can be found published in paperback, Kindle

He lives with his wife and best friend, their beautiful daughter, and their cat, Lovecraft.